HITLER'S
ANGEL

HITLER'S ANGEL

A NOVEL

KRIS RUSCH

MAX CRIME

Published by

MA☒CRIME

an imprint of John Blake Publishing Ltd,
3 Bramber Court, 2 Bramber Road,
London W14 9PB, England

www.johnblakepublishing.co.uk

First published in hardback in the United States of America
by St. Martin's Press, New York, 1998
This UK paperback edition published 2010

ISBN: 978 1 84454 928 3

British Library Cataloguing-in-Publication Data:

A catalogue record for this book is available from the British Library.

Design by www.envydesign.co.uk

Printed in Great Britain by CPI Bookmarque, Croydon CRO 4TD

1 3 5 7 9 10 8 6 4 2

Papers used by John Blake Publishing are natural, recyclable products made from
wood grown in sustainable forests. The manufacturing processes conform to the
environmental regulations of the country of origin.

MA☒CRIME series commissioning editor: Maxim Jakubowski

This one is in memory of Kent Patterson.

Acknowledgements

Thanks on this one go to Kent for the articles; to Nina, owner of the greatest German–American dictionary in the world; to my mother who always got 'the cart before the horse'; to Ron Rosenbaum and *Vanity Fair* in the Tina Brown years for publishing the article that started it all; and to Dean for everything.

ONE

Fritz pats his shirt pocket for his cigarettes. The pack is nearly empty, the cellophane crinkling beneath his fingers. The girl watches him, her wide, round American eyes taking in each movement. She perches on the edge of his metal kitchen chair. He has not risen from his seat. He doesn't want her to see that the orange plastic has ripped, revealing a mottled brown stuffing and the coil of a spring.

The apartment is bad enough: two rooms with a makeshift kitchen and a bath down the hall. He can afford better but he still sees luxury as a sign of schiebers and politicians — men who get rich off the pain of others. His money has come from the careful investment of his twenty-year-old windfall into television and business machines. He never speaks of those investments, made outside of Germany into American companies. He sees it all as vaguely illegal, although young Germans of today would probably applaud his foresight.

He pulls the cigarette slowly from the top of the pack and resists the urge to sniff the tobacco as if he held a Cuban cigar. His cigarettes are thin, wrapped in brown paper, and unfiltered. He read in the American propaganda he receives that such cigarettes can kill

1

a man – they have gone so far as to ban television advertising of all cigarettes in the United States – but they seem to have no effect on him. His fingertips are stained with nicotine, but his hands are unrecognisable to him anyway – thick, covered with tufts of white hair, with deep wrinkles. They look like his grandfather's hands, the hands of a man who died before this century, now in its seventy-second year, was born.

'You Americans all act as if the Demmelmayer case is the only thing that happened in Bavaria in 1929.' He grabs the matches off his scarred end table. He flips open the match lid, pauses, and adds with only a touch of sarcasm, 'There was a worldwide financial collapse in 1929.'

'The Demmelmayer case was important to police work,' the girl says. Her German is slightly accented. If he struggles, he can separate out the American inflections and discover how many of her teachers were Bavarian, Prussian, Pomeranian – or just plain ignorant.

With a single movement, he rips out a match. 'I have already talked about Demmelmayer. To schoolboys in the Fifties, BBC commentators in the Sixties, and now to you. Someone wrote an entire book on the case. You can find all you need in there. You do not need to speak to me. I have no more to say.'

'People have written about the case's sensationalism,' she says. 'I am studying how it fits into the science of crime-solving. For my dissertation.'

He studies her a moment. Americans have flooded Munich all spring to prepare for the Olympics, and to see West Germany. She is no different. She has taken advantage of the cheap airplane tickets to do primary research on her doctoral dissertation, and she hounded him until he finally agreed to this interview. He still isn't

2

sure he should have let her into the apartment. When she came to the door, he stared at her in dumbfounded awe, unable to speak for nearly a moment.

The round doe eyes. The high cheekbones. The rich brownish blonde hair. She is a ghost from his past returned.

Until she speaks.

'No one has examined the importance of your role,' she says.

He blinks, still astounded at her uncanny resemblance to a woman fifty years dead. 'What is your name again?' he asks, more to clear his mind than to refresh his memory.

'Annie. Annie Pohlmann.'

'Well, Miss Annie Pohlmann, they have all looked at the importance of the investigator. I have been a celebrity twice for this case. Once when I solved it, and then again when your Mr Hitchcock considered Demmelmayer as a base for one of his films.'

'I know about that.' Her voice is soft. 'He was never able to get a script he liked.'

'The case was not dramatic enough for him.' Fritz turns the match over in his hand. He remembers the man. Rotund, very British. A bit too interested in the graphic details. Fritz could not confide in Hitchcock, even though he had another story that might have interested the filmmaker. But despite their failure to work together, word of Hitchcock's interest was enough for articles on Demmelmayer, then a book, and later a bad television film, all of which gave Fritz enough money to last the rest of his life.

The girl shakes her head. 'Perhaps I am not communicating this clearly. I am writing about the way the inspector's mind works, the way it puts the details together. I believe that only certain people can solve certain crimes.'

3

She doesn't know how right she is. He puts the cigarette in his mouth. 'And then what?'

'What do you mean?'

'After the crime is solved. It is like a movie, no? To your American senses. The crime is solved and all is well.'

She glances at the room, at its shabbiness, and her cheeks flush. She thinks he is talking about wealth.

He is not.

'I expect it took a toll on you,' she says politely.

'What did?'

'Demmelmayer.'

He snorts, the idea absurd, and with a flick of his thumb, lights the match. 'And what led you to that conclusion?'

'You retired soon after.'

'No.' The match burns down to his fingertips. He shakes it out. The unlit cigarette bobs against his lips as he speaks. 'I worked another three years. No one remembers that. No one speaks of it.'

'Under Hitler?'

'I thought you were an historian,' he snaps.

'Of police procedures. I have no interest in Nazi Germany.'

He stares at her a moment, astounded that she believes she can study one part of a culture without studying another. The procedures he used, the procedures he changed, evolved because he was German, because he had been a soldier, because he had starved.

Because of Gisela.

He takes a deep breath, says, 'Hitler did not come to power until 1933. What do they teach you in your American schools?'

'Apparently not enough.' She speaks with a touch of wry humour, as if she knows her education is lacking.

4

'Then you should know that the Nazis introduced many new police techniques.'

'None I want to study,' she says.

'Because you shock easily?'

She shakes her head. 'I do not believe in studying the deeds of evil men.'

He strikes another match and, with a shaking hand, lights his cigarette. 'You know a man's heart, then?'

She frowns, swallows, and in an unconscious gesture, draws her bag closer to her body. 'None of the histories say you were a Nazi.'

'Many men go to great lengths to hide their past.' He takes a drag. The nicotine is cool against his throat.

'So you were.'

He shakes his head. 'I was in England by then.'

'But you believed –?'

'It is not as simple as that.' He stubs out the cigarette, disappointment filling him. Despite her looks, despite her curiosity, she is the wrong one. 'You do not need to talk to me.'

She lets her bag fall. It thuds against the floor. His sudden refusal seems to have intrigued her. She glances at the tape recorder she has set on the table beside her. A strand of brown hair falls across her face. He is wrong calling her a girl. She is a woman of perhaps thirty years. Old enough to have children of her own. Old enough to write books about things she does not understand.

She brings her head back up, looks directly at him. 'You worked for three more years,' she says, her doe eyes full of compassion. 'Yet no one speaks of it.'

He does not move. Her words catch him, her expression holds him. In it, there is something he has waited a long time to see.

5

'Why does no one speak of it?' she asks.

The air is full of a sudden tension. The question he has waited almost four decades to hear.

'Because they do not think it important,' he says. The words are a test. The final test. If she passes it, he will talk to her.

'And you do.'

He takes another cigarette, presses its end against the half-smoked butt, using the old cigarette to light the new. Then he takes a puff, letting the acrid, unfiltered taste burn the back of his throat. He releases the smoke through his nostrils. The white wisps curl around his face, obscuring her and the tiny, shabby room. 'I think,' he says, pulling the cigarette from his mouth, 'the things people fail to talk about are always the most important, don't you?'

The smoke clears. He puts the cigarette on his ash tray. She tucks the loose strand of hair behind her ear. Americans all have a fresh-faced look, an innocence bred of good food and adequate medical care. She seems to have no response.

He sighs. For a moment, he thought she would be the one. But she has shown she is not. For a moment, though, he believed....

He stubs out the cigarette. The interview is over, and he wants a glass of beer. He tried to speak to her, but like the last, she is not willing to listen. Well, then. Perhaps the next. Or the next.

Please God, he hopes someone will listen before he dies.

'Will you tell me why you quit?' she asks, her voice soft.

His breath catches in his throat. He wishes he has not put out his cigarette. He tries not to sound too eager when he says, 'If you listen to the whole story.'

6

TWO

The Föhn was still blowing when he arrived at Prinzregentenplaz. The wind carried dust from the gardens lining the buildings, off the cobbled streets, and into his eyes. He hated the Föhn – the wind some said brought hallucinations, and others claimed brought truth. Crime increased during the Föhn, a fact he always found odd, since the light Münich was so famous for was clearer when the strange wind blew down from the Alps. The Föhn had started the day before and had continued all night. And he had known, with a certainty that bordered on foresight, that change flew on this wind.

So he was not surprised to be called on a Saturday morning to one of the richest sections of the city, within walking distance of the *Englischer Garten*, the only peaceful place in the city. The few cars parked alongside the street were black and expensive, most of them Mercedes. The houses were Victorian, although some of the newer sported art nouveau facades. This block was full of apartment buildings, built for luxury, many two and three centuries old.

He stood in front of 16 Prinzregentenplaz, hands in the

pockets of his overcoat. So far, only the men from his unit and the street police had arrived. Good. With a murder in a location like this, the political inspectors could not be far behind.

*

'At this time,' he says, uncertain now about her level of knowledge, 'the Bavarian police had three divisions. The Schutzpolizei or the –'

'Schupo,' she says, as if to prove herself. 'They were what my country would call the beat police officers, the street patrol.'

'They were more than that,' he says, 'but it will do.' Then he waits. She smiles.

'There was also the political police or the Abteilung IA –'

'That was Berlin,' he says. 'Each German region had different laws, different organisations.'

'Not that different,' she says. 'There were political police in Bavaria.' He nods. 'Indeed, but we had another name for them.'

She frowns. 'What?'

'Assholes.'

Her grin is crooked. It makes her face her own. 'You were in the criminal police, and I know it was called Kriminalpolizei or the Kripo.'

'It was,' he says.

'So the Kripo and the Schupo were there, and you were expecting the assholes.'

'But they had not yet arrived.' He leans back in his chair and continues.

*

The building was imposing: five storeys high, with oriel windows and balconies from the second storey up. Gargoyles

8

hung over the windows on the second floor, their grinning faces malevolent, their stone eyes taking in all around them. The curtains were closed on all but the attic windows: he could see nothing inside.

Fritz took a deep breath before entering. He had had six homicide rotations since he solved the most famous case in Munich. Each time, everyone from the Government Councilor to the Chief Inspector had expected him to catch the murderer within hours of the crime's commission. He had, much to his own surprise – never confessed to the toll the job was taking on his dreams, and his nightmares. In his waking moments, he feared the next case, worried that he would not solve it, worried that this time it would steal his sanity completely.

This one was making him even more uncomfortable. Each case they handed him had a different degree of difficulty. The location of this one alone brought it into a whole new level.

Four stairs led to the main door. A constable blocked it, as he would in a crowded crime scene. Only here he fended off no one. Fritz took the stairs two at a time, his new boots shiny despite the dust. 'Where?' he asked.

'Second floor,' the constable said.

Fritz nodded and entered. The building smelled of polish, boot black and leather. The first floor held offices and smaller apartments. Another constable blocked the formal staircase. From somewhere above Fritz, a woman's voice rose and fell, not keening but nearly so. The voice held so much anguish, he could feel an echo in his own bones.

He passed the second constable, gripped the polished railing, and climbed wide staircase like the young man he no longer was. He remained trim, although he no longer had to qualify for police athletics. Still, he felt that someday his great physical condition would save his life – and it nearly had in August, when he lost his footing in a riot sparked by a Communist rally outside the Hofbrauhaus.

When he reached the second floor he let go of the railing and paused a final time. His heart was pounding. He would fail this investigation if he did not concentrate, but he did not want to concentrate. The woman's cry had awakened ancient ghosts in him as well.

The apartment covered the entire second floor. The landing was a brief stop for the other tenants to take before climbing to their own *gran luxe* apartments on the upper floor. The door to the second floor apartment was open, though, and from inside came the wail. The woman was actually speaking to someone in the sing-song voice of grief. He could hear mumbled male replies, barely audible, in response.

Fritz slipped inside the open door and nearly gasped at the richness before him. The floor was so well polished that it shined. Deep blue Oriental carpets began inside the foyer. Heavy curtains covering the nearest windows were in a matching blue, as were the deep-cushioned sofas. Oil paintings hung on the wall, the work dark and realistic. A few amateurish watercolours were mixed in, looking childish and out of place. The tables were made of mahogany – as highly polished as the floor. A pair of black leather

10

gloves had been tossed onto the occasional table beside the door. They provided the only clutter in the otherwise pristine room.

A stout woman in her late forties sat on the couch, her hands over her face. A sergeant Fritz did not recognise sat across from her, speaking softly. She was sobbing now, her wails having ceased.

Another woman stood behind the sofa, hands on its back. She watched Fritz, her eyes dark in her wrinkled face. Her hair was piled on her head, and her mouth was a flat line.

The sergeant looked up. His expression was much more open than the woman's.

'Detective Inspector Stecher,' Fritz said.

'I know who you are,' the sergeant said. 'Your problem is down the hall.'

Fritz frowned at the choice of words, but said nothing. Instead he followed the dark blue runner, looking for, and finding, traces of blood.

The unease he had felt on the street grew.

The rooms on the street side of the apartment were spacious and echoed the same design as the foyer. All of the curtains were closed, and some of the lights were on, making it feel like night indoors.

The drops of blood grew into blots as he approached the end of the corridor. Another constable stood near the door, arms crossed, straining the shoulders of his greatcoat. He stared straight ahead as if the watercolour above the mahogany table fascinated him. Fritz glanced at the painting: buildings and stairways in old Vienna, done in

11

stone browns and greens. The precise lettering on the posters hanging from a gate suggested a young artist's reluctance to use his imagination.

The trail on the runner ended near the constable's scuffed black boots. The blood went inward, through the door itself, into what appeared to be a bedroom.

'Detective Inspector –'

'Yes,' the constable said. He was young, the neck strap from his helmet pushing up his chin. He smiled as if the movement hurt him. 'You won't like this.'

Fritz didn't like it. He hated that the Schupo knew him and he didn't know them. It made him wonder how many people on the street recognised him from the stiff drawings of him the papers had printed when they covered his cases.

He stepped inside, braced for the smell. Blood, sickly sweet and pungent, but not nearly as strong as he had expected. Old. A dead body had an odour all its own, but blood, blood was the scent of a newly minted crime scene.

The blood trail led to a stain at the base of a dark blue fainting couch. He crouched. The stain was huge – almost three feet in width and two in length. The edges were dry, but when he pressed on the middle of the stain, blood welled, black and moist. Someone had died here. No one could lose this much blood and live.

He stood. Curtains covered a single window next to a bed made with military precision. Flowers stood on the nightstands. A door adjoined this room with the one next to it, and in the space between the extra door and the wall stood another end table, this one older and made of cheap wood. Above it hung a formal photograph of Adolf Hitler, head of the NSDAP, the National Socialist German Worker's Party. The man's face was thinner than it appeared in person, but the camera had managed to capture the intensity of the eyes. Fritz turned away, hating this reminder that the political police would want a piece of this investigation.

A dressing table stood beside the fainting couch. Perfume bottles crowded against a wavy mirror. A matching hairbrush and comb still had strands of dark brown hair clinging to them. In the centre of the dressing table, a fountain pen lay across a curling piece of paper. The chair was pushed back at an odd angle, making it appear as if whoever sat in it had been interrupted.

Fritz turned to the constable. 'Where's the body?'

The constable bit his lower lip. 'Gone, sir.'

'Gone?'

'Yes, sir.' Colour stained the constable's cheeks. 'It was gone when we arrived.'

'And the gun?'

'There was no gun, either, sir.'

Fritz sucked in a mouthful of the heavy air, wishing for a cigarette. 'All right, Constable. Bring me your sergeant.'

'Yes, sir.' The constable walked along the edge of the runner, careful to avoid the blood stains.

Fritz rubbed a hand over his face. Now he knew why they had sent him, even though he was one case away from his rotation in Inspectorate A, the Homicide unit. No other detective on the force had the reputation he had for solving difficult crimes. The techniques he had used first in

Demmelmayer had become standard in Munich, but they were *his* techniques – no one else on the force seemed to have the ability to see details and piece them together the way Fritz did.

All he had been told was that a woman had been shot to death at 16 Prinzregentenplaz. The Chief Inspector had stared at Fritz with an urgency, an intensity, as if he had expected Fritz to gather information just from the address. Fritz had shrugged and said that he was always cautious about crimes committed in wealthy neighborhoods.

He clasped his hands behind his back and walked around the sofa, noting that small traces of blood – too tiny to be called drops; more like a fine mist – had landed on the carpet behind. He avoided those and stopped beside the dressing table. Keeping his hands behind his back, he peered at the piece of paper beneath the fountain pen.

The pen had left a blot of ink on the bottom of the sheet. Above it someone had written in a flowing script: *When I come to Vienna, hopefully very soon – we'll drive together to Semmering an–*

Not a suicide note. He wasn't even sure it was written by the dead woman. He wasn't sure who the dead woman was – or if she was.

'Sir?' The sergeant he had seen earlier blocked the doorway, making the room seem dark. Fritz realised then that the only light came from one of the nightstands.

'Tell me why we were called here.'

The sergeant was a large man. His blond hair stood in tufts, as if removing his helmet had pulled up the strands. His eyes were small and buried in the flesh that threatened to overwhelm his face. 'The housekeeper says a girl was shot. Such cases always go to the criminal police.'

'You never saw the body?'

'No, sir.'

'You were first on site?'

'No, sir. Constable Wolfermann, whom you saw at the door below, he arrived first. When the housekeeper said someone had been shot, he sent for me. I called the Kripo.'

'Did Constable Wolfermann see the body?'

'No, sir.'

Fritz let out a hiss of air. Behind his back, he clenched his fists. 'So we have blood and a supposed body. With all the deaths and riots in Munich, you believed this to be important?'

The sergeant licked his lips, swallowed, and then said, 'The dead girl, sir. The dead girl, she is Herr Hitler's niece.'

THREE

'I *don't understand,'* the girl says. *'When you started telling me* *this story, you said no one thought it was important. This is* *about Hitler's niece!'*

This will be more difficult than he thought. *'In those days,'* Fritz says, *'Hitler was one of many small political leaders. We did not know what he would become.'*

'But clearly the sergeant understood this case is important. So is it? Or isn't it?'

Fritz clenches his left hand. He doesn't like Americans. They are so blunt and so demanding. *'You said you would let me tell the whole story.'*

'But what is this about?' she says. *'It can't be about Hitler.'*

'You said you would listen.'

'But if he'd done such a thing, he would never have been elected to office.'

'You are such an American,' Fritz snaps. Then he makes himself take a deep breath, makes himself calm down. *'This story is not about elections. It is about a crime. The most difficult crime I was ever assigned.'*

'More difficult than Demmelmayer.'

17

'Infinitely.' He runs a hand through his thinning hair. 'I would like a beer. Would you like a beer?'

She glances at the tape recorder, frowning in the failing light. 'I only brought one cassette. How long is this story?'

How long does it take a man to describe the end of his meaningful existence? One hour? Two? A day? A week? 'Long,' he says.

'Then why don't we finish up the investigation part today, and you can tell me the conclusions tomorrow.'

'It is not that simple,' he says. He needs something to do with his hands. He picks up the match box and turns it over and over between his fingers. Perhaps he has picked the wrong person to tell the story to. And it isn't just her lack of history, her naive American beliefs in simple, clear justice. 'You have never investigated crimes.'

He makes the question a statement, always, even now, pretending to know the answers in order to draw them out of his companion.

'That's right. I've never investigated anything except history.' She grins. 'I don't know how the history of the police in the West even became my specialty. Too many episodes of Alfred Hitchcock Presents, I guess.'

'So you only study technique. You do not practice it.'

She reaches to her left and pushes a button on the tape recorder. The faint whirring hum that has accompanied their conversation – a hum he hadn't been aware of until now – stops. 'I don't even study technique, really. I'm more interested in cases. I first read about Demmelmayer when I was a little girl. I have always wanted to meet you, to write my book on Demmelmayer. The definitive book. But I wanted it to read like a murder mystery. But the dissertation has to come first.'

18

'So you see me as a real life Sherlock Holmes?'

'I'm afraid so.' Colour touches her cheeks, adding to her healthy appearance. 'Silly, huh?'

'And if I turn out to be less than brilliant, you will still write this book?'

The surprise runs from her eyes to her hands. Her eyes widen, then her mouth opens and her hands nervously clutch her denim-clad knees. 'You would like me to write about you? I thought I could only write about Demmelmayer, but you're right. A biography would be even better.'

'No,' he says, the idea of recounting his life every afternoon until his death making his throat dry. 'Stick to your cases. But feature this one as a counterpoint to Demmelmayer.'

'They don't even sound similar.' The girl's frown is back, a feature of her concentration. She would make a terrible criminal. He can read her even in the growing darkness. 'At least in Demmelmayer, you had a body.'

'At heart, Demmelmayer was a simple case. Too many suspects, but no nuances. I had to eliminate possible killers, track motives, use any evidence I could find. In reality, though, Demmelmayer was no more than a domestic homicide. The case became famous because Gustav Demmelmayer was famous.'

'Adolf Hitler is famous,' she says.

'Now he is infamous,' Fritz says. 'Then, no one had heard of him outside of Germany. Certainly not Americans.'

He tries to say the word without contempt. But she doesn't seem to notice. She has pushed a button on the tape recorder again. She tried to be circumspect but he saw the movement.

So she is intrigued again. Good. That makes his job easier.

19

Although he must still explain the obvious to her, why he thinks this case a counterpoint to Demmelmayer.

He says, 'The Raubal case is full of nuance, and everything about it is hidden. Everything. But it fits into your hypothesis. No one else would have finished this case. You will want it for your dissertation. Then you can decide later if you still want to write your book.'

He stands, knowing she won't be able to see the hole in his chair in the darkness. 'I would like a beer. Would you?'

'Yes, one,' she says. 'And when I am done, I will have to go.'

'We won't finish tonight,' he says.

'I don't mind.' With the rush of words, he can almost feel her growing heart rate, the prickle under the skin, the excitement of the challenge. He remembers the feeling. He had felt it, underneath his anger, that morning in Prinzregentenplaz.

FOUR

Fritz's fists clenched so hard, his short-cropped nails dug into his palms. But he kept his face impassive. He didn't want the sergeant to see his frustration.

Adolf Hitler was a national figure with terrifying connections. His party, the National Socialist German Workers Party, had grown in popularity during the last few years. Its representation in the Reichstag had grown from 12 to 107 seats just the year before, and there was talk on the streets of Munich that Hitler himself would run for Chancellor in 1932. No wonder the Chief Inspector had looked at Fritz so oddly when he mentioned Prinzregentenplaz; just the week before they had been discussing how a man could go from being an impoverished enemy of the state to an influential politician who lived in one of Munich's most coveted neighborhoods.

'They say he is backed by the Kaiser's son, August Wilhelm.'

Fritz blinked, as much with surprise as a refocus on his concentration. The sergeant was making small talk.

'It doesn't matter,' Fritz said. 'We are a democracy now.'

The sergeant sputtered. 'And who would believe it? Last week –'

'You spoke to the housekeeper?' Fritz would not discuss politics. Not now. Not ever. Especially not with a member of the Schupo, whose politics could run with anything from the NSDAP to the Communists.

The sergeant straightened. 'Briefly.'

'When I came in?'

'No. I was speaking to another servant.'

Fritz tilted his head back slightly. He was behind in this investigation. He had been behind from the moment he entered the building.

'Where is the body?' Fritz's tone was getting sharper. He hoped it would mask the fear he felt like a thrum beneath his skin. This was the case. This one would defeat him. This one would prove that Munich's *wünderkind* was a man after all.

Unless he grabbed control now.

'I don't know where the body is,' the sergeant said. His eyes were shining. He wiped his hands on his uniform. 'I'm just a street officer, sir. I have never had criminal training – '

'Surely you're smart enough to know that one cannot have a murder without a body.' Fritz took a deep breath to calm himself. Yelling at the sergeant would do him no good. 'Did you ask what happened to the body?'

'The housekeeper called one of Hitler's men to open this door. Apparently it was locked. When he saw the body, he took it.'

'And do we know who this man is?'

The sergeant looked down. 'You'll need to talk with the housekeeper, sir.'

'I will do that. You're dismissed, sergeant.'

The sergeant nodded, then backed out of the room. Fritz did not watch him go. Instead he unclenched his fists and let his hands drop at his side. He was viewing a staged scene. The body was missing. Yet the household had been in such turmoil they summoned a constable, the lowest rank in Schupo, off the street, instead of calling for help from the Kripo. Deliberate? He didn't know. But he didn't like the situation.

Still, he would get his people to work the room, the entire apartment. He would interview the witnesses. He would need someone to guard them so that they couldn't change any story they had. Because his first priority was finding that body before it disappeared for good.

*

A click snaps him back to the present. The room is dark except for the light filtering in from the street lights outside the window. The girl's face is a ghostly reflection of itself. She smiles apologetically. 'My tape has ended.'

He nods, then waves her away.

She stands hesitantly. 'Would you like some light?'

He shakes his head. These memories belong in the darkness.

'Maybe we could go for some dinner?' Her voice trails off. She doesn't want to. She clearly feels sorry for him.

'I will see you tomorrow, precisely at eight. Bring coffee and pastries. I like plenty of frosting.' He makes his tone light.

'Will… will you be all right?'

He sighs. She will not leave him until he proves that he is fine. She seems to think the memories have disturbed him. Or that he is an old and frail man.

He is old.

He is not frail.

He snaps on the light beside his chair, blinking at the sudden brightness. 'I have been alone most of my life. Another night will not hurt me.'

She glances around the room as if she has not seen it before. And it does look different in the artificial light. The framed photographs on the walls do not cover the water stains and peeling wallpaper. The light catches the specks of dirt on the picture glass, specks that obscure each photograph. He has seen them all a hundred times. He no longer needs to look, but she seems to.

'At eight,' he says. 'Frosting.'

'Yes, right.' She runs a hand through her long brown hair, then grabs her bag and slings it over her shoulder. It lands with a thump against her back as she leans over to get her recorder. She makes a slight, almost inaudible grunt as she lifts it.

'Tomorrow,' she says, backing toward the door. Has he misread her? Does he look frightening in the dark? An athletic old man with a fierce face? Is that why she continues to watch him instead of turning her back on him? She puts her hand behind her and turns the knob. As she lets herself out, she calls, 'Good night.'

He does not reply. The door closes with a click. He drinks the last sip out of his beer glass — an ancient stein he stole from the Cafe Heck on a dare — then sets it down. The apartment is too quiet. The American has left him with his ghosts.

Before he even thinks, he is across the room, picking up the receiver on the phone bolted to the kitchen wall. His index finger barely fits in the dial's holes. He listens as the rotor turns, reflecting the size of each number he dials, but as he reaches the last one, he stops.

The last time he called, it cost him half a month's rent for a scrawny blonde who did not know how to apply false eyelashes, and who wore pantyhose instead of silk stockings. When he complained, he was told that the girls met his fantasy out of courtesy because he was a long-time customer, but silk stockings were expensive, and no one really remembered what the 1920s were like, now, did they?

He hangs up the receiver and leans against the plastic countertop. If he is honest with himself, he knows it is not the pantyhose that distracted him. It is the ancient look in the girl's eyes, a look he does not remember in Gisela's. When he was younger, he could ignore the look or pretend it was not there. But he sees everything now, in his old age, as clearly as if it were blown in on the Föhn. And if he is really honest with himself, he will remember that by the time she left in January of 1923, Gisela's eyes had no look at all. They were dead to everything but her own fear.

The dishes in the sink have the faint odour of soured milk. He needs to eat something, but he does not want to eat alone. Nor does he want more conversation. The past tightens his throat, churns his stomach. He will go to the beer hall down the block, eat sausage and sauerkraut, and drink until he cannot feel anymore.

25

FIVE

By the time he left the apartment, five members of his team had arrived. He only took the best of them – Henrich Felke, a detective sergeant who had worked well on previous cases. Fritz left four members on site: one to survey the crime scene, one to remove possible evidence, one to shepherd the witnesses to the precinct, and one to remain on the scene in case other people showed. Fritz spoke to the housekeeper enough to determine that Hitler had left after lunch the day before, and was not expected back all weekend. She did not know if anyone had informed him of the death.

The police coroner had offices near the police *präsidium* in the centre of town. When Fritz had become a member of Kripo in the mid-1920s, the coroner had also been a practicing doctor. But since the agitations of the last few years had risen, more and more of the coroner's work had been for the police. He now handled only murders and accidental deaths, sometimes five to ten a day.

The doctor's offices were in an ancient five-storey building. The grey stone was soot-stained, and the steps were worn in the centre. The building smelled of dust, old leather, and rubbing alcohol. Fritz always sneezed the moment he entered.

Henrich said nothing as he flanked Fritz down the long, arched hallway. When they reached the end they stopped in front of a wooden door with a frosted glass window. On the glass, in old German script, was the doctor's name: Gerhart Zehrt. Henrich gripped the cut-glass door knob and turned it. The door squeaked as it opened, the ever-present smell of formaldehyde mixing with the scents in the hall. The reception desk was empty, as it had been since Zehrt switched his practice to police work, but the door behind it, leading into the office, was open.

Zehrt was wiping off a wooden examining table. His sleeves were rolled up to show his massive arms. He was wearing a white shirt which loosely covered his round stomach. A blood-stained smock had been tossed onto the room's only chair. The walls were covered with glass-doored cabinets, revealing jars of medicines and canning jars filled with items that Fritz didn't want to speculate about.

'I have nothing here,' Zehrt said without looking at them.

Fritz stopped at the open door. His relationship with Zehrt had always been cordial, sometimes even friendly. They had the same attitude toward detail, the same desire to catch even the most common criminal. Zehrt had never stopped him at the door before.

'Henrich,' Fritz said, without looking at his assistant, 'I believe I left my cigarettes in the auto. Will you get them for me?'

28

Henrich nodded and clicked his boots together, a habit he had picked up from the soldiers in the department, even though he had been too young to serve in the war. He closed the outer door loudly as he left.

'I am looking for the body of a young woman. Her name is –' Fritz had to check his notes. The conversation with the housekeeper was more interesting for the information it lacked than the information he received '– Angela Maria Raubal. Also known as Geli. She would have been brought from Prinzregentenplaz.'

'I have no such body here,' Zehrt said. 'It's Saturday and the wife is making potato pancakes for lunch. I hope, this weekend, to get a chance to enjoy her cooking. No Communist marches, eh? No speeches. All quiet.'

The hair on the back of Fritz's neck prickled. 'I won't keep you. I just want to see the body. Then I'll be on my way.'

'There is no body here,' Zehrt said again. He continued wiping the faded and stained wood. His cloth was bloody.

'But you had a body here earlier, didn't you? That's why you're here this morning.'

Zehrt shrugged. He tossed the cloth on top of the smock, then went to the sink and washed his hands. 'Too many people die on Friday night. The wife would think I had a lover if she did not know better. I am never home on Friday nights.'

'I know you, Gerhart. You would have finished Friday night's work on Friday night.' Fritz crossed his arms. 'I was told that three men brought a body here this morning.'

Zehrt studied him a moment. They both knew Fritz would not leave until he had what he wanted.

'Two men,' Zehrt said. His voice came out softly, like a sigh. 'One dressed in the brown shirt of the National Socialist's private army, and the other, well, you know Franz Xaver Schwarz.'

Fritz did. Schwarz was the treasurer for the NSDAP. The Kripo had accompanied the political police more than once in an effort to determine where NSDAP was getting money to finance its new offices. Fritz had gone along on more than one of those visits.

'They called me. At home. I did not think it wise to say no.' Zehrt dried his hands on a thin towel hanging from a ring beside the sink. He gripped the edge of the counter and bowed his head. 'The body was already on the table when I arrived.'

Huge patches of sweat had dried under the arms of Zehrt's white shirt, leaving yellowish stains. Fritz had never seen the doctor look so dishevelled.

'You examined her?' Fritz asked. 'And she was dead?'

'Suicide,' Zehrt said. His voice had an odd strangled quality. 'That is my determination. Suicide.'

'How?'

Zehrt turned. His skin was grey, the lines deep around his mouth. 'A single gunshot wound through the heart.'

Fritz started. 'Through the heart?'

'Through the heart.'

'She lost a lot of blood for a single shot into the heart.'

For a moment, Fritz thought Zehrt wasn't going to answer. Then he said, 'The body was not discovered for some time.'

'Enough time to leave a stain three feet wide and two feet long?'

'I did not see where she was found,' Zehrt said.

'I did.' Fritz crossed his arms over his chest. 'You would have noted the blood loss.'

'The body had lividity in the rear extremeties,' Zehrt said. 'The remaining blood had settled.'

'She was on her back then,' Fritz said.

'So it would appear.'

'Shot through the heart, she landed on her back. She had an exit wound.'

'Yes.' Zehrt swallowed, his Adam's apple bobbing.

'She fell onto the carpet. Such an odd thing for a woman to do. One would think she would sit on the bed, put the gun to her temple, and shoot.'

'There is no understanding people,' Zehrt said.

'No,' Fritz said. Zehrt's nervousness was infecting him. 'There is no understanding people.'

'If that is all,' Zehrt said, 'I am expected at home —'

'Was the rest of the body untouched?' Fritz asked.

Zehrt turned around.

'The poor girl was very beautiful. Did you ever meet her? I did. Once. At the opera. She was laughing. You should see her.' Then he smiled. 'I mean you should have seen her. At the opera. So lovely.'

He picked up a piece of paper off the counter and crumpled it. 'Her mother is quite upset. The girl is to be buried in Vienna. They had a train to catch. Such a hurry to get the right papers. It is difficult to send a body across the border these days.'

31

He tossed the crumpled piece of paper into the empty metal wastebasket near the door. The basket pinged as the paper hit. 'I am going to finish cleaning up. The wife has lunch waiting. Would you mind helping with the trash?'

Fritz frowned. Zehrt never played games with him. Fritz went to the waste basket, plucked the crumpled paper, and shoved it in his pocket. 'You know, Gerhart,' he said, 'we do not drink beer as much as we used to.'

Zehrt rolled down his sleeves, but did not button the cuffs. 'I do not socialise much any more. The wife believes it is not good for my health.'

His gaze finally met Fritz's. Zehrt's eyes were dark, the pupils wide. He was not nervous. He was scared. Fritz had never seen Zehrt scared before.

'I thank you for the help with the clean-up,' Zehrt said. 'Now, if you'll excuse me, I must get home.'

Fritz nodded, and backed out of the office. He glanced at the windows, but saw nothing, no one watching. He hadn't had this feeling since 1919, just after the war, when a man had to watch his back at all times.

He let himself out of the office, and as he did, he heard the lock click behind him. He knew how the NSDAP stormtroopers could frighten. He had interrogated them for many of the violent crimes that Munich had seen in the last five years. But he had served alongside men just like them. They listened to authority. They thrived on fear.

Henrich was waiting at the car. He leaned against the driver's door, arms crossed. He was not wearing his uniform, and the sleeves of his shirt were too tight, leaving lines in his wrist. When he saw Fritz, he said, 'I couldn't find your cigarettes. I was wondering if you wanted me to buy you a pack.'

Fritz shook his head. 'I found them in my shirt pocket.'

He waved Henrich into the driver's seat, and Fritz let himself into the passenger side. He waited until the car pulled out before taking the crumpled paper from his pocket.

'So,' Henrich said, 'did he work on the girl?'

'He saw her. But he's afraid to talk about it.' Fritz smoothed the paper on his lap. 'Did you see anyone suspicious?'

'In Munich?'

They both laughed. Everyone looked suspicious these days. The city had taken a slight turn, and what had seemed like bohemian strangeness before the war now appeared to be a manic desire for control. No one listened any more, although everyone expressed an opinion. The opinions merely grew louder and more violent.

Henrich turned the car back toward Bogenhausen. 'Precinct?'

'Yes.' Fritz stared at the sheet of paper. It was dated 19 September 1931. That day's date. 'So, did you see anything?'

'No,' Henrich said. 'Not even people passing by.'

Which was strange in and of itself. Fritz frowned at the piece of paper. It was a letter. It read: *I have seen the body of Geli Raubal. She is, lamentably, a suicide. Please hasten the paperwork so that the body may be transported to Austria. The family would like to put her to rest outside of the public eye.*

It was signed by Franz Gürtner, the Bavarian Minister of Justice.

SIX

'*So many names,' the girl says. She has brought a notebook with her this morning, and is scribbling as Fritz speaks. A pile of cassette tapes sit beside her tape recorder, as if she expects him to talk all day. 'I do not know this one.'*

Fritz's fingers are wrapped around a glass cup filled with coffee and cream. The rich smell of the blend is more enticing than the pastries she has purchased from the faux German bakeries that cater to tourists. Next time he will tell her where to get real food.

The sun is warm on his back and shoulders. He has opened the curtains and straightened the apartment, no longer willing to be ashamed of where he lives. It took him most of the night, but it prevented the dreams.

'Some you will recognise. Some you will not. You will find all of the names in the papers of the day.' Fritz takes a sip of coffee. It is warm, bitter, and sweet at the same time. Soothing. 'We were all famous once.'

'I'm sure,' she says, patronising him. 'Go on.'

He sets the cup down next to the full ashtray. 'If you are uninterested, I can find someone else –'

'No!' she says quickly. 'I mean....'

She tucks a strand of hair behind her ear (her nervous gesture, he

35

notes), and sighs. 'This worries me, dealing with Hitler. I never expected to.'

'None of us ever expected to,' he says.

★

Fritz did not have time for meetings with the Chief Inspector. Fritz had a case to finish, witnesses to interview. But that was the message waiting for Fritz at the desk.

One of his men remained on the scene. The other three had returned, bringing evidence and witnesses. Fritz glanced over the preliminary list of seized evidence, noting that Hitler had a gun collection, although none of the weapons had been fired. Fritz let Henrich supervise the witnesses, keeping them safe until Fritz could question them. Then he headed to the Chief Inspector's office.

The office of the Chief Inspector had once been a hallway, but reorganisation in the precinct after the war had caused a redesign in the building. The exit leading to the alleyway had been sealed off and the hallway leading to that exit became a dead end. The walls were knocked out and a wall was built along the front, with a new door. The space was larger than any of the other offices, but it had never been repainted, and the grey walls served as a reminder of the room's former status. The Chief Inspector had covered the sealed-up door with posters announcing police charity events, and through the window which no one had bothered to remove were the bricks that now covered the back side of the building.

Fritz entered without knocking and closed the door behind him. The Chief Inspector was a slender man with a hawk-like nose who wore gold wire-rim glasses and kept his hair cropped short. He wore suits and ties, but never buttoned his sleeves, rolling the cuffs over the edges of the coat so that his wrists stuck out as if he were an overgrown schoolboy. His desk was littered with books, most taken from the shelves he had built on the new wall. A stack of papers teetered at the edge of the desk, and Fritz resisted the urge to straighten them.

'You knew,' Fritz said. 'You knew that the body was gone and that Gürtner was involved.'

'A crime was committed. We needed to look at it.' The Chief Inspector's blue eyes sparkled. He often worked Saturdays, but he rarely looked so cheerful about it.

'Gürtner says it was a suicide.'

The Chief Inspector folded his hands over the open book before him. 'What do you know of our friend Hitler?'

'I didn't know that he lived in Prinzregentenplaz until this morning.'

The Chief Inspector laughed. 'Ah, and I thought you did. I should have told you then.'

Fritz nodded. He lifted the books off the metal chair in front of the desk, looked at the Chief Inspector who said nothing, then set the books on the floor and sat on the chair. 'Our friend Hitler, his housekeeper says, is in Hamburg to give a speech.'

'Not just any speech. He is to kick off his presidential campaign at a rally tonight.' The Chief Inspector leaned forward. 'And how, you may ask, does a man imprisoned seven years ago for high treason, a crime that usually commands the death penalty, get out of jail within a year and become a national figure? No one knows, exactly, although some say that a certain Minister of Justice influenced the three judges hearing the case to be lenient. After all, Herr Hitler was following a moral imperative higher than the law.'

Fritz remembered hearing that argument before. Hitler's beer hall putsch in 1923 was known for its ineptness and for the egoism of its leader. Eighteen men died and a number more were wounded. But the loss of life didn't seem to matter, nor did Hitler's failure. Even the Schupo who had been in the crossfire swore that Hitler had the right to attack a weak and ineffective government.

No one was comfortable with the democracy forced upon Germany after the war. But that did not make treason right. The police knew that best; they were in charge of keeping the peace.

'Hitler has important friends,' Fritz said. 'Perhaps we should acknowledge that.'

'Oh, I do,' the Chief Inspector said. 'But Hitler was, as you say, out of town. Perhaps he does not yet know of his niece's death.'

'What are you saying?'

The Chief Inspector leaned back. 'I am speculating. Hitler has become an important man. A death occurred in his home. Such an event could be used to discredit him.'

'By whom?' Fritz asked, feeling cold.

'By anyone with motive.' The Chief Inspector's odd joy seemed to have grown.

'What do you want me to find?' Fritz asked.

'The truth,' the Chief Inspector said.

'There is no body,' Fritz said.

'The body is in Vienna,' the Chief Inspector said.

'But the Minister of Justice has already ruled. The girl died by her own hand.'

'Do you believe that?' the Chief Inspector asked.

'What I believe does not matter.'

'Nor does what you do when you are not working for the Kripo.'

Fritz's chill grew. 'Are you relieving me, sir?'

'Only for a short time. It seems to me that you need a vacation. I have heard that Austria is lovely in September.'

'Are you ordering me to do this, sir?'

'I believe you would be the best man for the task,' the Chief Inspector said.

'Will I have the backing of the Kripo?'

'You will have my backing,' the Chief Inspector said.

Fritz rubbed his hands along his knees. 'And if I see the girl in Austria, sir, and I believe the Minister of Justice is wrong? I will have to speak to Herr Hitler. I will have to talk with his sister, his associates. His housekeeper.'

'Hitler is used to police pressure. I am sure one Detective Inspector will not bother him over much.'

'He will tell the Minister of Justice. I will be breaking the law.'

'Then I will speak to the Minister of Justice.'

'And say what? That I am a wild man, that I do not belong in the department?'

The Chief Inspector smiled. 'I will merely tell him that you have a moral imperative higher than the law.'

'A moral imperative will not change the Minister's ruling.'

'No, but the truth might.'

'A man who can be bought cannot be swayed by the truth.'

The Chief Inspector pressed his fingers together. 'Ah, but there you are wrong, my friend. Such a man can be swayed by the truth when it threatens everything he has worked for.'

'So we are trying to protect Herr Hitler, then?'

'We are protecting no one,' the Chief Inspector said, 'except Bavaria herself.'

★

'Did you give him the letter?' the girl asks.

He feels a tension in his shoulders that he hasn't felt in forty years. The memory of that conversation terrifies him, although he was not afraid at the time.

In those days, he had known Hitler as a common, brutish politician: a small, loud Austrian who had managed to convince thugs and a few people in power to follow him.

Fritz had no idea what Hitler would become, what he was transforming into, even as the case unfolded. If he had known then what he learned later, he would not have pursued the case at all, despite the pressures put on him.

He would have politely declined, and faced the consequences.

'What?' Fritz asks the girl.

'The Chief Inspector. Did you give him the letter?' She is caught in the story now. She has stopped writing as he speaks, her notebook upside down and forgotten on the ground. She looks at her recorder only when it clicks and stops. He is relieved about that. He has chosen the right person after all.

Fritz holds up one finger, then pushes himself out of the chair.

He no longer cares if she sees the ripped back, the mottled brown stuffing, the ruined spring. She is seeing inside his life now. He can hide nothing from her if she is to understand.

As he walks into the bedroom, he hears a faint click. She has finally remembered to pause her recorder. He smiles.

The bedroom is dark. He still makes his bed military fashion, the corners precise, the blanket smooth and untouched. The room shows an obsessive neatness not reflected in the front room. His clothes hang in his closet, shirts arranged by sleeve length, suitcoats by age. The colours are all the same: blacks and whites. Only his First World War uniform tucked in the very back adds colour to the wardrobe. His police uniform and his undercover clothes are in the footlocker behind the shoes. He avoids it and instead pulls out a box of mildewing cardboard. He has not opened it in years, and he resists the urge to sit on his haunches and look through the memories.

Instead, he reaches inside and removes a cigar box sealed with brittle, yellow tape. He tucks the box under his arm and returns to the living room.

She is picking the edges off a pastry, avoiding the frosting and eating only the cake. She is studying her hands, but he caught the nervous glance she shot at the bedroom just before he came back. He returns to his chair, sets the box on his lap and slits the tape with his thumbnail. The lid flops open, flimsy with age. A pile of letters, still in their envelopes, line one side. He reaches to the bottom of the pile, to the only letter not in an envelope. The paper is still crinkled. The ink has faded, but Gürtner's signature is clear. He puts the box on the floor and hands the letter to her.

'My God.' Her hands shake as she takes the letter from him. 'My God.'

She stares at it for a moment, rereading it, realising (probably) that he can quote it from memory. This has been only a story to her until this moment. Now, though, she knows. She knows he tells her the truth. He can see it in her eyes, in her shaking hands. She looks at him over the paper's edge.

'May I take this with me?' she asks.

'No,' he says, unwilling, even forty years later to part with evidence. 'But you may photograph it here.'

She nods and, after a moment, hands the paper back to him. He folds it carefully and returns it to the bottom of the cigar box. She scribbles in her notebook, then adds a series of exclamation points. It irritates him that she writes her notes in English. If she wrote in German, he could read it upside down.

'Is there more in the box?' she asks.

He resists the urge to pick it up and clutch it to his chest. He had thought that speaking of this would be easy, like singing during an all-night drinking session. He did not expect this protectiveness, this odd, almost unclean feeling as he reveals his secrets. He cannot breach the past all at once. He must let it unfold, as much for himself as for her.

'There is more,' he says.

She waits. He stares at her. She has small lines around her eyes, a bit of facial hair beneath her chin. Finally she glances down at the box, and then at him.

'You do not have your recorder on,' he says.

She flushes and presses the play button. He grips the arms of his chair as he sinks back into his memories.

SEVEN

For a moment, Fritz hesitated outside the Chief Inspector's office. The Chief Inspector wanted him to go immediately to Austria, but that presented Fritz with a dilemma. If the Kripo did not conduct an official investigation, then no one would interview the witnesses. By the time Fritz returned from Austria, the witnesses would have time to change their stories, to disappear, or to refuse him.

He had to speak to them now. They had already spoken to each other, he was already sure of that, but he wanted one quick impression, some idea of what he was really up against, before he followed a corpse to Vienna.

The witnesses were waiting at separate desks, far enough apart that they could not speak to each other, but they could still see each other. The older woman's face was lined with tears. The matron sat ramrod straight in her chair, watching each movement in the precinct. And there was much to watch. Detectives flowed from desk to desk, carrying papers, discussing cases. The room was large and draughty. Fritz hated working here, often taking folders to a nearby café to study. As many as twenty detectives could

43

be working in the room at the same time. The conversations alone were deafening.

Henrich was seated behind one of the metal desks, studying an empty folder. He stood at attention when Fritz entered the room, a secret joke between them which dated back to the previous case. Fritz hated to be an authority, hated any signs of authority, so Henrich chose each moment he could to play on that hatred.

Fritz signalled Henrich to come closer, and backed into the hallway for some privacy. 'It is a suicide,' Fritz said. 'The case is closed.'

'But we haven't even seen the body yet,' Henrich said. 'How can there be no investigation?'

'I didn't say that,' Fritz said. 'Occasionally, I will need your help. Off-duty. And no one else's.'

Then he paused and ran a hand through his short-cropped hair. What he was going to ask next was not proper, but Henrich's answer would be critical to the case.

'Forgive me,' Fritz said, 'but if you belong to NSDAP, I need to know now.'

Henrich blinked as if the question shocked him. 'I have no party affiliations,' he said. 'You know that. We've discussed –'

'I know nothing. And someone leaves the NSDAP propaganda in this office, just like someone else leaves the Communist literature. I am merely making certain that it is not you. It matters only in that if you do have any affiliations at all, you will not need to spend your spare time with me.'

'And miss the warmth of your friendship?' Henrich smiled. 'I have no party cards. You may check my wallet, my apartment, or my leisure activities. You will find that I live in beer halls only because I cannot cook.'

Fritz nodded, more relieved than he cared to mention. Even so, he would have another detective double-check Henrich's statements. The secretive nature of this case had already infected Fritz's blood.

'I need to speak with the witnesses,' Fritz said. 'Alone. Bring me the older woman first, and then the housekeeper. I will be rather quick, as I have other business this afternoon. So watch. When I signal for the next, be ready. And, when they leave, do let them know that I will be needing to speak to them again.'

He did not wait for Henrich to answer. Instead he went down the hall to one of the interrogation rooms. The older offices had been remodelled into the rooms. They were little larger than walk-in closets, with none of the charm. A single unprotected light bulb hung above a sturdy metal table. The chairs were made of painted wood, and the windows had been boarded over long before. He took the first available room, pleased that it had been cleaned since the last time he used it. The single bulb illuminated the table but left shadows in the corners, shadows he paced away. He leaned against the boarded window while he waited for his first witness.

After a moment, Henrich opened the door. The stout woman entered. She walked with a slouch, her back already pushing up into a dowager's hump. Despite the warmth of the day she wore a homemade sweater over a cotton dress, and high button shoes that dated from before the war. Tears had left deep shadows under her eyes.

Fritz stepped forward and extended a chair for her. Henrich closed the door and disappeared down the hall.

'I am Detective Inspector Stecher,' Fritz said.

'Marlena Reichert,' the woman said, as she slipped into the chair. She did not meet his gaze.

'I have a few questions for you, Frau Reichert,' Fritz said. 'I understand that it has been a trying day.'

The woman nodded. Her dark hair was curled, and threaded with grey. She clutched a large bag to her chest.

'Do you work for Herr Hitler?'

'I help in the kitchen,' she said. 'And with other chores. Frau Winter is the housekeeper.'

'Where do you live, ma'am?'

'In the apartment,' she said softly. 'I share a room with my mother.'

'And is your mother here?'

'No,' Frau Reichert said. 'She is still in her room. She does not want to come out. It is a house of death, she says, and she says she will not leave the room until I find her somewhere else to stay.'

'A house of death?' Fritz asked.

'My mother,' Frau Reichert said softly, 'she is old.'

He pulled out the other chair, and sat on its flat seat. He did not need to intimidate this witness. She was upset enough as it is. 'Tell me what happened this morning.'

She clutched her bag tighter. 'My mother and I overslept. When I got up, Geli was not out of bed. I got worried, and I tried the door to her room. It was locked. She did not answer my knocks, so I finally called Herr

46

Schwarz. He came with Herr Amman, and together they broke down the door.'

Zehrt had mentioned Schwarz. Fritz made a mental note of both names and watched her as she spoke. Her hands twisted the handle of her bag, over and over, bending and scarring the leather.

'Then what happened?' he prompted.

'She was – at the foot of her sofa, in her blue nightdress, still holding the gun. The wound was tiny in the front, but the blood –' Tears filled the woman's eyes.

'You were close to Geli?' Fritz asked, watching the tears, remembering the woman's deep grief in the apartment.

'No,' the woman said. 'No.'

Her response surprised him. He had thought she was in mourning. He would come back to this. 'What position was she in?'

Frau Reichert opened the clasp of her bag and retrieved a wadded handkerchief. She wiped at her eyes. 'She was on her back, her eyes open. She looked so surprised.'

'Was it her gun?'

Frau Reichert shook her head. 'It was one of Herr Hitler's. He kept a collection in his room.'

'Where is the gun now?'

She shrugged. 'I do not know. I did not go back to her room after they took her away.'

'Did you hear anything? A gunshot? Any shouting?'

'Not in the night.'

'In the morning?'

'No,' Frau Reichert said.

'Was there a note?'

Frau Reichert shrugged. 'I did not go into the room. The men went in.'

'What made you call Herr Schwarz? Didn't you have a key?'

She glanced up at him, quickly, then down again. 'I – I was worried,' she said.

'But you didn't care for Geli.'

'She is – was – trouble.' Frau Reichert opened her handbag and put the damp handkerchief back inside. Then she whispered, 'God forgive me.'

'Trouble?' Fritz asked.

'Herr Hitler did not permit her to go out. Munich is dangerous, he says, and he is right. And she would not listen to him. She said she had no one after the bird died.'

'Bird?'

'Hansi. Her canary. She wouldn't let us bury it.'

'When did the bird die?'

Frau Reichert snapped her bag closed. 'Not long ago.'

'Why do you think Geli died?' He waited for the answer. He purposely did not mention suicide.

Frau Reichert stared at her hands. 'She was willful. Capricious. She never listened.'

'She killed herself because she never listened?' Fritz asked.

Frau Reichert lifted her head. The tears had formed again. Her lower lip trembled.

'I didn't hear anything,' she said, and he realised that from the way she spoke, she was not referring to the gunshot. Something had happened. Something else was going on, and she was trying, in her inefficient way, to hide it.

48

The trip to Vienna might not be wasted after all.

'What happened after you found the body?'

'I don't know,' Frau Reichert said.

'You don't know what you did?'

'I went and told my mother. She heard nothing either.'

'When did you come out of your room?'

'When Frau Winter arrived with the constable.'

'Frau Winter lives on site as well?'

'No. She went home last night.'

'Who called her?'

Frau Reichert shrugged. 'I was with my mother.'

Fritz bit back his frustration. The woman was terrified, but he did not know if she was terrified of him. She was old enough to remember some of the excesses after the war, but not everyone viewed the police with fear.

'Where was Herr Hitler this morning?'

'I don't know,' Frau Reichert said. 'He was to give a speech, but I don't know where. Not Bavaria. They don't let him speak in Bavaria. The restrictions are unfair, he says.'

'Where can he speak?'

'He spoke in Berlin.' She shook her head. 'I don't know much about his business.'

'When did he leave?' Fritz asked.

'Yesterday. Afternoon. After lunch.'

'Are you sure?'

'Yes,' she said.

'Did he have lunch with Geli?'

'Spaghetti,' Frau Reichert said. 'Geli said she was sick of spaghetti. But he loves it, you know.'

'When did she say she was sick of spaghetti?'

'Yesterday.' Frau Reichert's voice had lowered. She wiped at her eyes with the back of her hand.

'Were they fighting?'

'She wanted to go to Vienna. Ungrateful girl. She has everything right there.'

He noted the shift to present tense. Frau Reichert had said those words before. 'Is that what they fought about?'

'He didn't want her to go. He had called her back from the last trip. But she was yelling at him.'

'Did you hear what they said?'

Frau Reichert shook her head. 'Not after I served the spaghetti. They yelled all through lunch.'

'Then?'

'He left. And she went into her room. I know because she slammed the door so hard the walls shook.'

She could hear a slammed door but not a gunshot. Fritz said nothing about that. 'And then what happened?'

'Nothing. I did not see her.' Frau Reichert swallowed and looked at Fritz. 'Until this morning.'

A tear ran down the side of her face and remained under her chin. She did not wipe it away.

'Why are you crying?' he asked softly.

The tears fell hard now. She bit her lower lip, then opened her bag and removed the crumpled handkerchief again. 'I don't know,' she whispered. 'I don't know.'

EIGHT

*F*ritz takes a breath. 'I need a cigarette,' he says. He is out.
He is hoping she will offer to buy him a pack, although he
refuses to ask.

She looks at her watch. It is round and gold with tiny roman
numerals on its face. A slender hand ticks away each second. He cannot
read the watch upside down either. 'We should probably have lunch.'

'There is a deli down the block.' He does not offer to buy them
lunch. He wants her to bring the food back. He wants her to leave
him alone for a few minutes.

She grabs her bag, stands. 'I'll buy.'

He does not rise. 'I would like cold roast pork on salt rye. And a
pack of cigarettes. Tell them the cigarettes are for me. They keep a
carton for me under the counter.'

She opens her mouth, closes it, and smiles. The smile does not
reach her eyes. 'I thought perhaps we could talk.'

'My dear,' he says, 'I have been talking.'

'No, I mean, about me.'

He looks at her, really looks at her, in a way he hasn't wanted
to. Her pantsuit is umber polyester, her bag plastic. She has worn the
same white platform shoes every day since he met her. She is not

51

part of the workers, the opportunists who have come here for the Olympics. Such a travesty that will be. They have ruined his city, rebuilt it with their ugly designs, and they think that such an event can erase the bloodstains of the past.

Just as Hitler thought in 1936.

But this woman, this Annie, she is not one of them. Despite her inadequate history, her poor education, she is here to discover things. To dig up the past. The Olympics made a trip to Munich affordable, she said to him on the telephone when she arrived. She is on sabbatical, she has told him that, but she probably came to Munich alone, studies alone, spends her time alone. Her grant is probably small, and her income from her teaching position smaller. After she leaves him, she returns to the apartment the university provides for her and studies in the silence, away from her friends, her family, her world.

He sighs, then pulls his wallet from the drawer of the end table. He hands it to her without counting the bills. He knows how much money is in it, knows how much lunch will cost.

'I am an old man,' he says softly, knowing it is an ersatz excuse. 'I need a moment to rest.'

Her smile remains, but the edges of her eyes pinch. He has hurt her.

'Please,' he says, 'buy whatever you like.'

'I should pay. You're helping me.'

He lets the words hang in the air for a moment. He is not sure who is helping whom. Then he smiles and waves her away. 'You bought breakfast.'

She nods, turns, but not before her smile fades. She looks older today. She lets herself out, and he waits until he can no longer hear her footsteps on the stairs. Then he gets up, like a sleepwalker, and returns to his bedroom.

52

He has left the cardboard box in the middle of the floor. He crouches, and reaches inside. The cardboard squeaks as the back of his hands rub against the sides. His fingers brush mounting board, and even before he has a chance to think, the photograph is in his hands.

It is the wrong photograph. This one he has forgotten. It hits him like a fist in the belly. He stares at the posed photograph, taken of his family just before he left. His younger self stands straight and sombre, his uniform loose, its collar starched, the gold buttons looking white in the black-and-white print. His hat is tucked under his left arm, his chin is jutted forward. He has a young, hopeful look that disappeared in the trenches. None of his later photographs ever seemed so bright-eyed.

But it is not his younger self that hurts him. Nor is it Gisela. She is even more beautiful than he remembered, her brown hair piled on top of her head, her smile soft and serene. She wore no make-up in those days, and her black dress, although simple, accentuates the fullness of her figure in ways the cabaret clothes she favoured in the Twenties never did.

No. It is not his wife that stops his heart. It is the babe she cradles in her arms. Wilhelm. Fritz never lets himself think about Wilhelm.

Footsteps on the stairs. He tosses the photograph back in the box, then folds down the flaps and shoves the box back into the closet. He pauses, puts a hand over his forehead, presses against the bridge of his nose. Even then, the image will not go away. The one that he sees in his dreams. Little Wilhelm, named by an idealistic youth for his precious and misguided Kaiser. Wilhelm, whose face was so thin when he died that he looked like a skeleton already.

She knocks, then opens the door. He stands, almost losing his balance.

'Frederich?' she says. 'Herr Stecher?'

He makes himself walk to the door. 'Fritz,' he says. 'Since we are spending our days together.'

She smiles, a real smile this time. She pulls a box of cigarettes from the bag she carries, and hands them to him. Then she goes into his kitchen and takes dishes from the drying rack. She arranges the sandwiches on two plates as he watches. A woman has not worked in his kitchen, not in the two decades that he has lived here.

'The deli is quaint,' she says.

Quaint. The warmth he felt toward her recedes. Quaint. A condescending word. So that he cannot forget the political hegemony that separates them. He would never call anything American quaint.

'It has stood on that corner longer than you have had a homeland,' he says.

'Well,' she says, unconcerned by his tone, 'it certainly seems authentic.'

She hands him his plate. He takes it and sets it beside his chair. She takes her sandwich and sits. He goes back into the kitchen and pours himself a beer. It is early to be drinking.

It is late to be thinking of Wilhelm.

But he does both.

'So,' the girl says, her mouth full of food. 'Did the housekeeper confirm Frau Reichert's story?'

He grips the counter, marvelling how one part of his past can save him from dwelling on another, darker, infinitely more terrifying part.

NINE

The housekeeper, Frau Annie Winter, did not hunch. Each movement she made had a military precision. The wary look she had had in the apartment had hardened into a craftiness that he trusted even less. She sat in the same chair Frau Reichert had, but Frau Winter used it like a battle station to counteract his every move.

During his brief interview with her in the apartment, she had seemed distracted. Here she had a sharp focus as if the few hours that had gone by solidified events in her mind.

Fritz did not sit when he spoke to her. Instead he stood over her, crossing his arms and standing as close as he could without touching her. Those who intimidate hated to be intimidated.

'When did you go to the apartment today, Frau Winter?' he asked.

She looked up, met his gaze evenly. 'Frau Reichert called me. She wanted the keys to Geli's room.'

'Why didn't Frau Reichert have keys?'

'She is responsible for no one except her mother.'

'What is their position in the household?'

'They are guests of Herr Hitler.'

'They are family then?'

'No.' Frau Winter's mouth was tight with disapproval. 'Frau Reichert was his landlady before he moved to Prinzregentenplaz. She was kind to him. He is kind in return.'

Fritz clasped his hands behind his back. The room had a chill dampness that seeped from the brick. 'So she does nothing to help you.'

'Oh, she helps. When it amuses her,' Frau Winter said. Her tone was even, her face impassive.

'You don't like her.'

'What I like or don't like doesn't matter,' she said. 'Geli is dead.'

She glanced at him again, as if to make certain he caught the rebuke. He did, and thought it interesting. Witnesses usually responded in anger or fear. Frau Winter merely added to the chill. 'Did you see the body?'

'No,' she said. 'They already had it in the car when I arrived.'

'Whose car?'

She blinked and small frown lines appeared on her forehead. The pause was slight but, he felt, significant. 'I do not know.'

'Herr Schwarz's car? Herr Amman's? Herr Röhm?'

She brought her head up sharply. Behind the chill in her eyes was something else, something darker. Anger? Or fear? 'Röhm was not there.'

Fritz nodded, once, formally. 'My mistake. I had heard that a Brownshirt was present. I assumed it was Herr Röhm.'

'Who told you a stormtrooper was there?'

No one had told him. He was guessing. But it seemed logical since one had appeared at Zehrt's. Hitler's people trusted the Brownshirts more than they trusted anyone else, especially the Munich police.

Fritz moved closer, so close he could smell the soap she had used. 'If you did not see the body, how do you know that Geli is dead?'

'Frau Reichert saw it. She told me.'

'Couldn't she have been mistaken? She doesn't seem like a very competent woman.'

'She's not. She is only in the household because of Herr Hitler's generosity.' The fact seemed to bother Frau Winter. She did not approve of Hitler's living arrangements.

'Frau Reichert and her mother are impoverished?'

'No, they own still apartments on Thierschstrasse.'

He stored that piece of information as something to explore later. 'But she is not very competent?'

'She burned sausages yesterday. She blamed in on the Föhn.'

'So why did you believe her when she said Geli was dead?'

Frau Winter's mouth set in a straight line. She knew she had been trapped, and she wasn't pleased with it. 'Because, Detective Inspector, there are certain things which are impossible even for a *dumkopf* to miss. Geli was dead.'

'And Herr Amann and Schwarz also believed this?'

'Yes.'

She had not volunteered information. She had merely confirmed it. It still left the mystery of the SA man. 'What did you do when you arrived?'

'I saw that the household was in disorder. I had seen a constable on the street and I sent for him. Then I calmed Frau Reichert, and Frau Dachs –'

57

'Frau Dachs?'

'Frau Reichert's mother. I sent her to her room. And then I looked in Geli's room. Such blood.' Frau Winter shook her head. 'I did not touch anything.'

'I thought Frau Dachs didn't see anything.'

Frau Winter shrugged. 'I do not know what she saw and what she didn't.'

'I would like to speak to her.'

Frau Winter waved a hand. 'She is old,' she said, in a tone that meant *she is crazy*.

They had kept the old woman from him. He would have to remedy that, or have Henrich do so while he was away. He still wasn't sure how involved he wanted Henrich to get.

'Why did they take the body?' Fritz asked.

'I don't know,' she said. 'They were leaving as I was arriving.'

'So you did see them take the body.'

'No,' she said. 'It was already in the car.'

'How did they get it there?' he asked.

Her gaze was level. 'They carried it.'

'In a blanket?'

'I did not ask.'

'But you're the housekeeper. Wouldn't you know if they had taken something?'

She raised her chin slightly. 'You saw the apartment this morning, Detective Inspector. It will take me days to return it to order.'

He leaned on the table. 'What was their manner when you saw them? Did they think Geli was still alive? Is that why they left so quickly?'

58

'No,' she said. 'I think they wanted Geli properly cared for. Herr Hitler would want that.'

'Herr Hitler.' Fritz backed away a little. He was gripped his hands so tight, pain tingled through his fingers. 'Geli Raubal was his niece?'

'Yes.'

'And where are her parents?'

'Her father is dead. Her mother runs Herr Hitler's home in Obersalzberg.'

'Does her mother know?'

'I phoned her, yes.'

'And does Herr Hitler know?'

'I do not know. He is on his way to Hamburg.'

'Couldn't you phone him as well?'

'He was to arrive in Hamburg today.'

'So he left late yesterday.'

Frau Winter's mouth became a straight line again. She had caught him before he completely sprung the trap this time. The woman was sharp. 'He left just after luncheon.'

'Did he lunch with Geli?'

'Spaghetti. His favourite.'

'Were they getting along?'

'Ach,' Frau Winter said, waving her hand dismissively. 'No one got along with that girl.'

'No one?'

'She was flighty. Dissatisfied. He gave her everything.'

'Could someone have killed her?'

'She was still holding the gun when they opened the locked door.'

'But you brought the keys. How did they get into the room?'

'They broke the door down.'

'Who told you that Geli was still holding the gun?'

'Frau Reichert.'

'Who can't be trusted.'

Frau Winter sighed as if Fritz were an exasperating child. 'The girl killed herself.'

'How do you know that?'

'Because she was despondent.'

'All the time?'

'Yesterday. After he left. She found the letter.'

'Letter?'

'From another girl. In Herr Hitler's coat pocket.'

Fritz felt off balance himself. 'And such a letter made her despondent?'

'She wanted to become Gnädige Frau Hitler. He is highly eligible.'

Fritz started. He had not expected this. 'But she was his niece.'

Frau Winter shrugged. 'She flirted with everyone.'

'So then a letter from another girl would not have mattered.'

'It mattered.' Frau Winter frowned and shifted in her seat. 'She wanted to be the most important person to everyone who was near her. It would have made her more important to marry Herr Hitler. He is an important man.'

Fritz swallowed. He had not thought of this. 'Where is this letter now?'

'She tore it up.'

'Is it still in the apartment?'

'Yes,' Frau Winter said.

'I would like it,' Fritz said.

'I will make sure you get it,' Frau Winter said. Her acquiescence surprised him after the difficulty she had given him about Frau Dachs. The Chief Inspector was right to have suspicions. But suspicions of whom? Of what? The behaviour around this death led Fritz to believe that Geli Raubal did not commit suicide. But she might have. Even that would be embarrassing to a man with political ambitions.

'I do not understand,' Fritz said, trying to weave through the tangles to the truth, 'why such a thing would drive a girl to kill herself.'

'She was possessive, jealous. She wanted Herr Hitler to herself.'

'Was he her lover?'

'No!' Frau Winter's cheeks coloured. 'He was like a father to her. He only wanted to protect her.'

'From what?'

'His life has been hard. He did not want hers to be.'

'She was jealous and possessive, yet flirtatious and flighty. I do not understand, Frau Winter, how you knew her heart.'

'She was an impulsive, thoughtless girl. She probably picked up Herr Hitler's gun and in a moment of rage turned it on herself.'

'Yes,' Fritz said. 'The gun. Where is it now?'

'It was in her hand.'

'I know.' Fritz kept his voice level. 'But it was gone from the room when I arrived.'

Frau Winter's eyes narrowed just a little, as if she were weighing him before she responded. 'Perhaps they could not get it from her hand.'

'Perhaps?'

'I do not know what they did with the gun,' she snapped.

'You said Geli probably picked up the gun and turned it on herself. There was no note then?'

'I did not see any.'

'And the gun belonged to Herr Hitler?'

'All the guns in the apartment belong to Herr Hitler. He was a soldier, you know.'

No, Fritz had not known that. But it did not surprise him. Most men in Munich had served in the war. 'How many guns does Herr Hitler have?'

'He has a collection.'

Fritz knew. He had seen it. Hitler seemed to have a passion for guns. 'And Geli knew where the guns were stored?'

'He keeps them in a glass cabinet. We all know where they are.'

They all knew. Fritz suppressed a sigh. This case was twisting him and he did not have the resources he needed. Damn the Chief Inspector. Damn the Minister of Justice. Fritz needed a team to work this. Someone to examine the evidence, another to chase the body, a third to grill the witnesses, and a fourth to find Herr Hitler. 'So you arrived, saw the broken door, and called the constable.'

The thin mouth again. 'I was appalled they had not done so sooner. After all, the girl was dead. The police would have to be involved.'

She was very astute. Get the police involved before they got themselves involved.

'Tell me again the sequence of events.'

She sighed. 'I arrived. The door was broken, Frau Reichert was crying, and the men had taken Geli to the car. I saw the blood, and knew that we had trouble. That girl thought of no one but herself.'

Fritz decided that the chill in the room had nothing to do with the bricks. 'No sadness at Geli's death? Did you dislike the girl?'

Frau Winter met his gaze. 'Geli was a woman past 21–'

Fritz stared. Somehow he had assumed she was younger.

'– and she used that womanliness to her advantage, distracting Herr Hitler and disrupting the household.'

'Did she disrupt the household yesterday?'

'She disrupted the household every day.'

'What happened yesterday?'

'She wanted to go to Vienna. She has been wanting to go to Vienna for weeks. Herr Hitler has told her no, that she cannot go, but still she wants. They fought over lunch.'

'Did the fight get violent?'

Frau Winter laughed. 'You cannot make Herr Hitler the villain here. He was long gone by the time Geli died.'

The denial was interesting. Fritz had not been trying to make Hitler the villain. He had been trying to see if there was a cause of suicide.

'How do you know when Geli died?' Fritz asked quietly.

'She was alive when I left after I made dinner. Herr Hitler

was already on his way to Hamburg. He left in his Mercedes immediately after luncheon.'

'Frau Winter,' Fritz said, leaning forward and speaking with great respect, 'who told you that Geli committed suicide?'

Again, the brief hesitation, the slight frown. 'Everyone who saw her.'

'And who would that be?'

'Frau Reichert, Max Amann, Franz Schwarz.'

'You spoke to the men, but were unable to see the body?'

'They already had her in the car. They did not want anyone gawking at her.'

'Where did they take her body in such a hurry, Frau Winter?'

'To a doctor, of course,' she snapped.

'But she was dead.'

'They still needed papers to get her out of the country.'

'Out of the country,' he said as if he had not known. He had learned long ago the importance of double-checking facts. 'Where?'

'Her mother wants her buried in Vienna.'

'Did you speak with her mother?'

'Yes.' Frau Winter's voice lowered. 'She was distraught, the poor woman. Blaming herself.'

'And she was in Obersalzberg?'

Frau Winter's mouth thinned. The woman's movements were small, but telling. 'She was.'

'When did you speak with her?'

'This morning.'

'Before or after you sent for the constable?'

'During,' Frau Winter said. 'I sent one of the servants for the constable while I called Frau Raubal.'

'Where will they bury her?'

'The Hitlers are Catholic,' Frau Winter said. 'They have had a long relationship with Father Pant in Vienna.'

'How do you know Geli has been sent there?'

For the first time, Frau Winter bowed her head. Her hand shook as she used it to smooth her hair.

'How do you know, Frau Winter?'

'Because,' she said softly, 'Geli is a suicide. It will take family connections to get her buried at all.'

TEN

*F*ritz pushes himself out of the chair. His throat is dry. He hadn't realised talking would be such an effort. He steps into the small kitchen, intent on getting himself more beer. But he cannot drink too much while he speaks. He must keep his mind clear. Instead, he has one of the American sodas the girl has brought.

She is watching him. He holds up the can, offering her some, but she shakes her head. He pours the soda into a thin glass without ice and watches the drink foam. That makes him think of beer, which makes him a different, uncontrollable kind of thirsty, and he has already rejected that. So he returns to his chair with his drink.

She is frowning. Her frowns are elaborate things, so unlike Frau Winter's. Her round face puckers, her features shift. Frau Winter only moved a small wrinkle over the bridge of her nose.

'Did you know what Frau Winter meant when she said that about family connections?' the girl asked.

He set his glass down beside the full ashtray. Ashes have spilled on the blonde wood, staining it. He will have to clean again. 'You were raised Protestant?'

She smiles. 'My parents did not believe in religion.'

His hand pauses over the table. He had met Communists who claimed not to have religion, but never anyone else.

'It's allowed in America,' she says, 'to believe whatever you want.'

Her tone has a subtle shade of judgement. All Americans do when they speak of religion, as if Germans do not understand tolerance.

Perhaps they don't. The history doesn't show it. In fact, very few people he knew showed tolerance. Even now.

She leans forward. For a moment, he thinks she is going to touch him. He does not move.

'So,' she says. 'What did she mean by family connections?'

'To Catholics, suicide is an unpardonable act. The victims are placed in unconsecrated ground. Often a priest will not conduct the funeral. Angela Raubal's family sent her body to a priest who knew her, who would probably be willing to, in the least, beg God's mercy for her soul.' Fritz is grateful to be talking again, grateful the awkward moment is over, grateful that she has given him a way to continue gracefully.

'I think I read about that practice somewhere,' she says, her smile back. 'Religion makes people do strange things sometimes.'

'Yes,' he says with more sadness than he intends. 'Yes, it does.'

*

The daylight was fading when Fritz emerged from the precinct. If he wanted to find the body, he would have to go to Vienna. Even if he left now, he would drive all night.

Fritz stopped beside his car and rubbed the tension in his neck. He would have to go now. The family would appear for the funeral. He needed to arrive first. He wanted to view the body privately, to examine it for any clues he could find.

He had got another detective to use the precinct's

telephone to contact the priest. The parish apparently had a telephone as well, but the priest was as averse to its use as Fritz was. The detective's conversation was short and loud, but he did manage to confirm a day and time for the funeral. It would take place on Monday in the morning.

So few hours for Fritz to be alone with Geli, to see what secrets she would share before taking them with her to the grave. At least he had those few hours. Frau Winter's mention of Father Pant meant that Fritz was not spending his evening with train schedules and porters, asking who had taken the body of Geli Raubal out of the country.

Fritz got into the car, and placed his overnight bag beside him on the front seat. He kept extra changes of clothes at the precinct, often because he was not able to go home at night, and he preferred to wear clean clothes even if he had not slept. Those were the clothes he packed for his trip to Vienna. Next to the bag, he placed the department's camera. It was large, awkward and square. It took both hands to hold it. But he had become accustomed to it. It had been useful in several other investigations. He had taken it for this investigation without asking.

As he pulled away from the curb and flicked on the headlights, he felt more alone than he had felt since he joined the Kripo. To do this case properly, he should stay in Munich, interview the men who spirited the body away, find Hitler, see the letter Frau Winter had mentioned, speak to Frau Dachs, and discover the history of Geli's relationships with the people around her. But he could do nothing without viewing the body. All he had so far were innuendoes of murder. If it became clear, after his trip to Vienna, that the girl's death was an odd and politically embarrassing suicide, Fritz would speak to the Chief Inspector and asked to be released from the case.

Without even realising what he had done, he found himself on Prinzregentenplaz. He glanced at the buildings, shadowy in the growing dark, then pulled over in front of Geli's apartment building. If he left now, he would arrive in Vienna before dawn. The trip over the mountains was treacherous in the daytime. At night, it would be more so, and it would slow him down. But it did not matter if he arrived in Vienna at 3 a.m. or 5 a.m. Either way, he would get his work done. He had a few moments, then, to see if Frau Winter had returned to the apartment. If she had, she could give him the letter before he left. He might also be able to see Frau Dachs. It was better than waiting until he returned.

A small crowd of curiosity seekers had gathered in front of the main door. They stood silently, almost worshipfully, as if expecting someone. He passed through the crowd and let himself in, surprised that the main entrance was not locked. The lights on the stairs were dim; the building's owner had replaced gas lights with electricity but had tried to keep the same fixtures. The place looked ominous in the shadows.

The door to Geli's apartment was closed. Fritz listened, but heard nothing. He was not surprised; the apartments here were built for silence. He had noted that morning the door was as thick as his arm.

He knocked. The sound was weak in the padded hallway, and he would have backed away at that moment if something in Frau Winter's tale of the letter hadn't nagged at him. Part of him was convinced that the letter did not exist.

He was about to knock again when the door flew inward. A small man, his hair dark and slicked back, his face puffy and white, stared intently at Fritz.

'Go away,' the man said.

Fritz nodded a greeting. 'I am Detective Inspector –'

'I don't care if you are Hindenburg himself. Go away.' The small man spoke with such force that spittle sprayed Fritz. He did not back away. Instead, he placed a hand on the door frame.

'I am Detective Inspector Stecher. I am investigating the death –'

'Of Geli,' the little man finished. 'There is nothing to investigate.'

He started to close the door, but Fritz reached above the little man's head and held the door open. As he looked down, he suddenly realised whom he was standing before.

Adolf Hitler, head of the NSDAP, rumoured presidential candidate, and uncle to Geli Raubal. Fritz felt a shock run through him. Since he had last seen Hitler, the man had put on weight. His moustache was filled with food particles and his hair was dirty. His clothing was rumpled, and his eyes were swollen. It looked as if he had been crying.

Fritz had never seen Hitler so distraught. The man had always been a fireball of anger and efficiency. Fritz left his hand on the door, but he softened his tone. 'I beg your pardon, Herr Hitler. The Kripo would like to close this case as quickly as possible. I –'

'Case? Case? There is no case. There is nothing for you here. Geli is dead.'

'I know,' Fritz said. 'But the Kripo must investigate all unnatural cases of death. I know this is difficult, but –'

'The Bavarian Minister of Justice has already determined that Geli committed suicide.'

'Yes, sir.' Fritz kept his tone even, although a great frustration was welling within him. 'But there are certain protocols that must be followed, even if a ruling has been made. If you would allow me to come inside, I will explain the procedures, and get through them as quickly as possible.'

Hitler's lower lip trembled. He let go of the door, and backed away. For a moment, Fritz thought he was going to be allowed inside. He too let go of the door.

Hitler shook his head and gazed down at the polished floor. He seemed very small, shrunken, as if the news had diminished him somehow. He was not the man Fritz had watched in the streets of Munich.

'I am sorry, Detective Inspector,' Hitler said. His voice had lost all the force he had used a moment ago. 'I have only just returned. My niece is dead. I simply cannot face talking with you at this hour. Perhaps in the morning…'

'I think it would be best for all of us to have this matter closed by tomorrow,' Fritz said.

'No,' Hitler said. He looked up. His eyes were large and glistening. The hall was full of the scent of his cologne mixed with the faint odour of sweat. 'No. We shall talk tomorrow, Inspector.'

And then he closed the door so swiftly that Fritz barely had time to move his hand off the frame.

Fritz stood before the door, staring at the carving in the wood. The apartment number had been etched in Gothic numerals. He could not hear any movement inside, and it almost felt as if Hitler were standing on the other side of the door, waiting for Fritz to move.

Fritz raised a hand to knock again, then decided against it. Best to go to Vienna, and see if he had a case at all.

ELEVEN

'You were kind to Adolf Hitler?' The girl sounds stunned. Her posture has shifted subtly and he can't quite read it.

'I treated him as I would have treated any witness,' Fritz says.

'That's not true,' she says. 'You wrote in the handbook you compiled after Demmelmayer that an inspector should never let a witness determine the time and place of questioning.'

The recorder clicks beside her. The tape is done.

Fritz sighs. He should never have compiled that handbook. Reporters, investigators, and rookie detectives have all quoted his words to him as if any violation of them was violation of sacred writ.

'I had unusual problems in this case,' he says. 'If I pressured Hitler, he would contact the Minister of Justice, who would then wonder why I was pursuing a closed investigation.'

The girl grabs a tape from the top of her stack, and slips it into the recorder. Then she closes the lid and hits the record button. When she looks at him, she smiles, as if she has caught him at something.

'That's not why you didn't pursue him,' she says. 'You didn't pursue him because at that point, you thought Geli had committed suicide.'

'No,' Fritz says. 'At that point, I hoped she had.'

He drove all night, across roads that were difficult for the alert driver. He pulled over for a short nap near the Austrian border, waking when the chill in the car grew too great. He arrived in the outskirts of Vienna before dawn and was at the church when the first mass of the morning had just ended.

It took no time to find Father Pant. The priest was younger than Fritz had expected – a thirtyish man, slender to the point of gauntness, with deep shadows under his eyes. He tried to hide his great height by slouching, which only made his body seem both tall and crooked. Father Pant was removing his vestments when Fritz entered the priest room behind the altar of the church, revealing a conservative black suit underneath.

'Forgive me, Father,' Fritz said, keeping his head down. He felt tired and rumpled. He had yet to find a hotel room and change. Instead, he had concentrated his efforts on finding the church. 'One of the altar boys told me where you would be. I'm Detective Inspector Stecher from Munich. I am here about Geli Raubal.'

The priest adjusted the collar and cuffs of his suit, then smoothed his hair. 'You arrived quickly, Detective Inspector. I am surprised at your haste. I thought that German police have no sway in Austria.'

Fritz nodded. He felt like an altar boy himself in this room, small and powerless next to the man before him. 'Of course not, Father, but I was wondering if you could help me. The family removed Geli's body before the police had a chance to see it, and we believe that the death may not have been a suicide.'

The priest was placing his robe on a hanger. He stopped

76

when Fritz said the word 'suicide'. For a moment, he stood with his back to Fritz, then turned his head slightly. 'I have documents from the Bavarian Minister of Justice and from a police doctor. Are you saying these documents are false?'

'No, Father. They're authentic. But the circumstances were unusual, and the doctor suggested, in a roundabout way, that I look at matters myself. By the time the Kripo had even been informed of the death, the body was on its way here.'

The priest finished adjusting his robe, then he hung it on a peg behind the door. 'I suppose you have papers?'

Fritz pulled out his identification papers, and showed them to the priest. The priest picked up a pair of half glasses off the table and held them in front of his eyes without attaching them to his ears. Then, with one hand, he folded the glasses, and with the other, he returned Fritz's papers.

'I have known the Raubals a long time,' the priest said. 'Angela, Geli's mother, was quite upset when she spoke with me yesterday.'

'She called you?'

The priest nodded. 'She will be here this afternoon.'

'Where is the body?' Fritz asked.

'At the Central Cemetery. No one arranged for a mortician, so I did.' The priest put his glasses in their case and stuck the case in his breast pocket. His hands were sure, his manner calm. 'The mortician will also arrive this afternoon.'

Fritz felt his mouth go dry. A mortician would alter the body – it was his job. Fritz waited for the priest to continue with his comments, but he did not. 'Have you another mass this morning?'

Father Pant shook his head. 'We have a nine a.m. mass and a noon mass, but I shall perform neither. I was going to use the time to prepare for tomorrow's services.' He took his long coat off the wall peg. 'Come along. We shall take my car. No one will remark upon it.'

'Thank you,' Fritz said. For all his matter-of-factness, the Father seemed as curious about the circumstances of Geli's death as Fritz was.

'No thanks needed,' Father Pant replied. 'I do this for Geli. Her soul is still my responsibility.'

*

A click stops him. The girl smiles at him apologetically. 'Something's wrong with the tape,' she says.

Fritz still wants a beer. A headache throbs at the back of his skull, has throbbed since he saw the photograph. 'This is a fine place to end,' he says. 'I will see you in the morning then.'

'Would you like me to bring breakfast again?' She has not even begun to pack her equipment. He wishes she would move. He wants to be alone.

'Yes, fine,' he says. Their relationship seems to be based on food. Of course, all of his relationships with women seemed to have revolved around food.

She nods, places her tapes in her large bag, and slings it over her shoulder. Then she picks up the recorder. 'Until tomorrow, then.'

'Until tomorrow,' he says.

She lets herself out, pulling the door closed quietly.

The endings of these sessions are awkward for him. He feels as if she expects something more from him. Entertainment? A quiet dinner? He does not know.

He stays in the chair as darkness grows around him. For years, he was afraid to speak of this, afraid to remind people that he was the one who had been forced to retire from the Kripo over the Raubal case. He had tried to speak then and was silenced. Then he did not speak at all. No one cared in London. When he returned to Germany, when he had his measure of fame, when he was ready to speak in the decades after the Second World War, no one wanted to listen. He had become a national hero, somehow, the man who had solved Demmelmayer, the man who had developed modern crime-solving techniques. The London Times *had called him 'Germany's Sherlock Holmes'. The* New York Times *had called him 'The Greatest Detective in the World'. Someone had discovered him, someone had claimed Fritz's reputation was great, and people believed him. Hitchcock had tried to make his film in 1950, and when that became news, all the Berlin newspapers contacted him. They contacted him again in the 1960s, after that abysmal television movie aired worldwide. Scholars started knocking on his door. Everyone made money from his fame, even him.*

Yet that has not bothered him. The dreams bother him. They are not of Demmelmayer — he only thinks of Demmelmayer when someone asks — but of Geli. In his dreams, she is laughing, a beautiful young girl, the kind that once looked at him with admiration and longing. Then a cloud passes over her face, and when she cries his name, the cry is full of terror.

He always awakens chilled, no matter how warm his rooms are. He makes himself tea, not coffee, after those dreams, and wraps himself in blankets, looking out of his windows at Munich after dark. With the chill comes a great guilt, a guilt he does not completely understand.

Over the years, the dream's frequency has increased. Soon he will have the dream every night. Every night, haunted by Geli. He will become as bad as Hitler whom, they say, made the dead girl his own private obsession. Fritz does not want that. He wants peace in his last few years. The only way he can have that peace, he believes, is to talk out the memory. Exorcise the dream. But try as he might, he has not found anyone who is willing to listen.

Until now.

This girl seems so frail, so fragile. Perhaps he asked her because she reminded him of Geli. But that can't be true. He has asked other scholars, men, to listen. They refused. The Raubal case made no difference in modern police science — their specialty, all of them. Only Demmelmayer made that kind of difference. Demmelmayer. A routine murder gone awry. Gustav Demmelmayer murdered his wife in a fit of passion. He had, however, covered his crime very well. Another detective, in an earlier time, would not have solved the case.

Fritz had, because he knew science. But more than that, he solved the case through his attention to detail, his interpretation of that detail, and his sideways knowledge of the human mind. Years later, when he had nothing to fill his days, he read the Sherlock Holmes stories by Arthur Conan Doyle, and was startled to discover that an English fiction writer had come up with the same idea decades before. Only he had never explained the techniques. They were accorded to Holmes' brilliance, to his own special insights — insights the average man could not have. Fritz had brilliance, no one argued with that. But unlike Holmes, Fritz had shared that brilliance in a way the most common detective could understand. For that, Fritz had become famous. For that, Fritz would be remembered in the annals of crime history.

Little comfort as he sits alone in his two rooms, in the dark, with dreams of a dead girl haunting his sleep. Little comfort at all.

TWELVE

The morning was grey and cold, reflecting Fritz's mood. The Central Cemetery was also grey and cold, with its stone fences and wrought iron gates. The mortuary inside the gate was empty. Father Pant parked his car around the back, and used a gold key to open the unpainted wooden door. Fritz brought the camera with him. It was heavy and large, and he had to carry it carefully. Father Pant watched him without offering help. The camera itself had gained a withering glance from him earlier when Fritz had removed it from his own car.

Inside, the mortuary smelled of decaying flowers. Father Pant bypassed the public rooms and took Fritz through a dark, unlit hallway. The air was cool here as well, as if someone had left the heat off, and the smell changed from dying flowers to the tang of formaldehyde. The smells seemed exaggerated, the silence heavy, and Fritz attributed his over reaction to his lack of sleep.

Finally, Father Pant led him to double doors made of cheap stained brown wood. The brown had faded near the knobs where pressure of hands had rubbed the stain away.

After Father Pant pushed the doors open, he reached for the light switch to the right.

Immediately a string of uncovered electric bulbs lit, banishing the dark. Fritz understood why Father Pant went for the light first. The room was the size of three normal rooms, with lockers standing against the far wall. There was a basin sink near the lockers, and counters ran along the remaining walls. Wooden tables filled the rest of the room, all stained dark, but even the colour could not hide the black blotches that irregularly marked each surface.

The body of an elderly woman, covered with a pale blue cloth, lay on a table closest to the lockers. Her silver hair draped across the side of the table, and the uneven ends brushed against the floor. Her eyes were open and sunken into her face, her mouth a silent 'O' of pain. Even the odour of formaldehyde could not hide the stench of rot.

Father Pant said nothing. Obviously he had been in the room before. He pointed to an unpainted wooden coffin beside one of the counters.

'That should be Geli,' he said.

'Have you seen her recently?' Fritz asked. 'Would you be able to recognise her?'

Father Pant nodded, but didn't move toward the coffin.

'I'm sorry,' Fritz said.

Father Pant shook his head and sighed. 'Sometimes I think God has cursed me, asking me to do his work during the last twenty years. The things I have seen....' His voice trailed away. Then he turned to Fritz, eyes dark with sorrow. 'Geli Raubal was an energetic girl, lighthearted, given to easy laughter. I cannot picture her dying by her own hand. I cannot picture her dying.'

The priest's words echoed in the large room. Fritz hadn't realised until then how much the other man's voice carried.

Fritz walked over to the coffin. It was cheap, obviously hastily put together for transport. The men who had taken the body had not had a coffin with them – or had they? Frau Winter had been unable to answer his question about the way the men transported the body. He should have asked Frau Reichert, but he hadn't thought of it. He would ask her, or the others, when he returned. He couldn't imagine even the most grief-stricken being willing to put a blood-soaked corpse flat across the back seat.

Someone had taped a piece of paper to the top of the coffin. It read 'Angela Marie Raubal', and had the address of the Central Cemetery in Vienna. Across the top was a stamp, marking the transportation paid. He took a photograph of the coffin's lid, then set the camera on the counter next to a pile of tools.

Fritz grabbed a hammer from the pile and prised the lid off the coffin. It took him a moment – the coffin had been sealed with a number of nails. Father Pant came up beside him and watched. The squeals of the wood and metal were the only sounds in the room.

The odour seeping from the coffin made Fritz's eyes water. Father Pant crouched beside him and helped him pull the lid off. The smell was overwhelming. Fritz put a hand over his nose and mouth, but too late. The stench had already coated his tongue and the back of his throat. He wouldn't have expected this kind of odour on someone who had been dead a little less than 24 hours.

'Merciful God,' Father Pant said. He was staring into the coffin.

Fritz stared as well. Geli had been a tall woman. She filled the coffin. Her blue nightgown had been pulled down over her thighs. A small round hole surrounded by powder burns was beneath her left breast. Fritz had expected that much.

He had not expected her face.

The area around her open eyes and her nose was black and blue. Her nose was flat, the skin swollen but not, it appeared, from the after effects of death. A bit of blood had dried beneath her nostrils. Her lips were cut, and she had another bruise beneath her left ear.

He had seen a woman he loved look like that.

He had touched her.

Gisela.

He closed his eyes for a brief moment, struggling for control. He had to think of the present, not the past. He had become a detective to blot the past from his mind.

He opened his eyes.

Zehrt had said that she had lividity in the back. The blood had settled. These wounds happened before she died.

Her hands were at her sides. Fritz leaned over the coffin. Three nails on her left hand had been broken, and had not been filed, even though the remaining two were perfect ovals. Her right hand hung at an unnatural angle from the wrist. Her bare legs were covered with yellow bruises above the knees, older bruises that had occurred days before her death.

'Merciful God,' Father Pant said again. 'The poor child.'

The poor woman. For Geli was a woman full grown, with a slender body and long well defined legs. Fritz could not tell if she had been beautiful. The damage was too severe for that.

'Father,' he said softly. 'I would like to check the rest of her body for injury.'

'I think that would be wise, my son.'

The familiar form of address surprised Fritz. Father Pant had been careful to call him 'Detective Inspector' before. They had gone from antagonists to conspirators in solving a woman's murder.

Fritz pushed up the nightgown, made of a soft satin, in a bizarre imitation of foreplay. Her skin beneath the satin was cold and rigid. His own action disgusted him. He was used to watching Dr Zehrt work on the corpses. He had never done so himself.

The bruises ran up Geli's legs and disappeared into her small black pubic thatch. Her waist was cross-hatched with red welts and a few scars. Her breasts and upper body were untouched.

'The doctor did not examine her,' Father Pant said.

'I think he had no choice but to sign that document,' Fritz said. He stood, and took the camera off the countertop. Father Pant said nothing, watching silently, his expression softer than it had been near the church. Fritz took as many photographs as he could, some of Geli's face, others focusing on her torso, still others on her legs. The flashes left red and green spots in front of his eyes. When he was finished, he set the camera back on the counter, then bent over and eased the nightgown back down, attempting to give Geli what dignity he could.

He had learned compassion since Gisela's death.

He shook his head. It was Geli before him. Geli, not Gisela. Gisela had been dead for years.

He turned Geli slightly and examined her back. The nightgown was black with blood, her limbs discoloured as the remaining blood settled, just like Zehrt had said.

The exit wound was as large as his fist.

But there was no gun. Not beside her body, not beneath it, and not in her hand.

He eased her down. There was no need to photograph her back. The evidence he needed was on her face and her legs.

He had just grabbed the coffin's lid when Father Pant touched his shoulder.

'What's that?' Father Pant asked. He crouched beside Fritz and pointed to the material near Geli's right breast. There, stuck into the satin, was a small, yellow feather.

'One of the servants said she had a canary,' Fritz said.

Father Pant nodded, and without saying a word, the men replaced the coffin lid. Fritz also pounded the nails back in place. No sense in alarming the mortician or the unknown persons (if any) who had accompanied the body.

'All morning I have worried about how to place her in consecrated ground,' Father Pant said. He looked at Fritz, his face grey in the odd light. 'I shall have no trouble doing so now.' He ran a hand on the coffin. 'Most merciful God.'

'God has never been merciful,' Fritz said. 'And He never will be.'

THIRTEEN

*F*ritz *smokes an entire pack of cigarettes before the girl arrives.*
He stands in the window and watches morning come to
Munich, the first pedestrians on the sidewalks, the first cars
speeding through the darkened streets. As the light comes, so does
the laughter and loud conversation, faint but reassuring through the
thick panes of his windows.

He slept only three hours, and during those hours he dreamed of
Geli. Not the Geli who has haunted him for years, but the Geli he
knew, the dead woman whom he touched ever so lightly so many
years ago. He knows he cannot speak of this properly, of the
elongated feel to the event, as if each minute lasted a day, nor can
he describe the physical reality of the smell. It had been another
presence in that room, a living reminder of the reality of death.

Father Pant had provided the only comfort, the only warmth, and
that too Fritz cannot relay. How does he tell a girl he does not know
about the faith he lost before the war? How does he explain that for
a brief moment, Father Pant's compassion revived that faith? The
priest's shock, horror, and concern revived similar emotions in Fritz,
emotions he thought long dead, buried with his son, but dying since
the war. He cannot explain how he needed to remind himself of

God's essential lack of caring, how often and how well God had shown his complete lack of mercy.

How Father Pant would have looked at him, at Fritz, if he had known, truly known, what sort of man Fritz was.

Fritz does not know how to explain the depth of his sudden feelings, the profound change Geli's corpse and the priest's humanity evoked in him. He has tried to find words for that experience since he awoke, but they are inadequate.

All of the horrible events of his life crystallised in that one moment and pointed the way to the future, to the gas chambers and death squads, the casual murders and the upcoming war itself. The atrocities, which some now saw as isolated, were part of a fabric, a thread, woven long before Hitler was born, long before any of them were born, and honed to a fineness in the years after the First World War.

Somewhere, somehow, the people around him took on a meanness, a lack of caring, a casual evil. And he had become so inured to it that it took a face like Geli Raubal's, a reaction like the priest's, to remind him that the world was meant to be different.

And yet it is not, even now. He stands at his window and hears the sound of construction not too far away. The Olympic Games, symbol of hope, an attempt to cover over that casual evil. But the evil will appear somewhere during the event He knows that. He does not know how. And if he were still a detective inspector, he would go to his chief and remind him that nothing is easy in this land. That an entire people do not unlearn hatred in less than a generation. That such hatred breeds extremism, not just in the Germans, but in everyone who contacts them.

Even the girl. Every time Fritz mentions Hitler, she shies back, as if she expects the man's ghost to appear in the room. 'I do not

88

believe in studying the deeds of evil men,' she has said, as if she had a choice, as if they all had a choice, as if closing one's eyes made all the evil go away.

Closing one's eyes only makes the evil thrive.

That is what he needs to tell her. Because in Geli Raubal's face he saw a reflection, a reflection of all he had closed his eyes to, a reflection of all he has tried to forget.

When the girl, Annie, does arrive, she brings pastries from the bakery he has pointed her to. They look fresh but he does not eat, wanting instead to speak of his dream, of his memory. He waits until she finishes, until her coffee is gone, and her tape recorder is in its place. Then slowly, carefully, he speaks the words he has rehearsed, watching her face as he does.

Her eyes are wide, her cheeks flushed. As he describes the extent of the wounds, the edges of her mouth tighten. She is not an investigator. In her life, she probably has seen few corpses. She probably has seen only photographs of murder victims.

He does not describe the smell.

When he is finished, she says, 'Why have I never heard of this case?'

Her voice shakes. Even though he has glossed over the details and has not spoken of his own change, he seems to have conveyed it. She is clearly moved. If she was not involved before, she is now.

'You have not heard of it,' he says, 'because you were not meant to.'

FOURTEEN

The hotel room that Fritz rented was tiny and damp. The radiator clinked as steam moved through it. The sheets on the bed were clean but the blanket was thin and full of cigarette burns. He took a short nap, and he was so exhausted that he did not dream. When the alarm clock awakened him, the sun was setting over the spires of the city.

Before going to dinner he returned to the church. Father Pant's car was parked at the rear. The windows overlooking the lot left squares of light on the gravel. The back door was unlocked, and Fritz went inside.

The church smelled of dust and candlewax. He had entered through a large kitchen. The white sinks and stove showed some recent money in the parish. Dishes still dried on the counter from the afternoon. In the distance, he heard voices, one of them a woman's.

He followed the voices through a dark hallway, finally finding another square of light spilling on the red carpet. The voices were louder now. He recognised Father Pant's, speaking softly. Then Fritz stepped into the light and rapped on the open door.

They were sitting in a study, Father Pant on a large red-upholstered chair, the woman on a couch. Theology books lined the walls, and behind Father Pant, a neat mahogany desk gleamed. Father Pant held a pipe and was twisting it round and round in his hands.

The woman was small. Her dark hair was piled on top of her head in a fashion years out of date. She wore a black dress with a single gold brooch. Her waist was surprisingly narrow for a middle-aged woman. Her short legs were tucked under her long skirt. Only the tips of her sturdy black shoes peeked out. Even though Fritz had never seen her before, he knew who she was.

Angela Raubal. Geli's mother.

If Geli had lived, she would have looked like this one day, a face of faded prettiness and quiet strength. Frau Raubal looked up at Fritz. Father Pant stood, said nothing about Fritz's unexpected arrival, and made the introductions. When he was done, Frau Raubal turned an unexpectedly intense gaze on Fritz.

'You're the man who says my daughter was murdered.'

Fritz stiffened, unwilling to look at Father Pant. Fritz had wanted to break the news to her, had wanted to see the look in her eyes the moment she knew. He wanted to know if she had faced the news with expectation, sorrow, or surprise. He stepped into the room, and uninvited, sat on the wooden chair beside her.

'I do not say, Frau Raubal.' He spoke softly, like Father Pant did, wanting to draw her into their conspiracy of knowledge instead of alienate her from it. 'I know. You would as well if you saw Geli.'

Frau Raubal glanced down at her hands. They were coarse, callused hands, the hands of a woman who had worked all her life. 'The Minister of Justice says Geli committed suicide.'

'The Minister of Justice has not seen her. He would have made a different ruling if he had seen the body.'

'Seen! Seen!' Frau Raubal glanced up, and her blue eyes caught him again, reminded him of someone he could not name. 'What is so important about seeing her? What happened to my little girl?'

Father Pant was watching him, hands carefully folded in his lap. Fritz was startled to realise the priest was wearing his robes. He apparently needed all the strength of his office to speak to this woman about her daughter's death.

Fritz took a deep breath. The woman was on an edge, and he needed her. He needed her to believe him to give his investigation strength. 'Forgive me, Frau Raubal, for being so blunt, but someone beat Geli before she died.'

Frau Raubal's face went white. The power in her gaze faded, and she seemed to retreat into herself. 'Beat her?'

'Yes, ma'am. The bruises she had could not have happened after death.'

'But they said she shot herself. Maybe when she fell —?'

'No.' Fritz kept his voice gentle. 'Bruises look different before death. And the body does not bleed afterward. Someone broke her nose, Frau Raubal, so close to her death that Geli did not have time to wipe the blood off her upper lip.'

Frau Raubal clasped her hands in her own lap. Her expression did not change, but her eyes took on a faraway look. Father Pant glanced at Fritz, as if surprised by Frau Raubal's reaction.

'Do you know what Geli did to provoke this?' Frau Raubal asked.

A chill ran down Fritz's back. He had not expected that question. It was not one he would have asked if it had been his child in that coffin at the cemetery.

Not now, anyway.

Perhaps a few years before.

Now he knew that people did not provoke beatings like that. Beatings like the one Geli Raubal suffered came from extreme rage. 'We don't know if she did anything. We don't know what happened. We were wondering if, perhaps, you knew.'

Frau Raubal bit her upper lip so hard that Fritz could see the pressure in her jaw. With a very small movement, she shook her head.

'Angela,' Father Pant said, 'we would like to help Geli.'

'There is no help for Geli,' Frau Raubal said. Her teeth had left marks in her lip. 'It was my mistake.'

'What was?' Fritz asked.

'Sending her so far away. To Munich. She was not ready to go.' Frau Raubal was staring slightly to the left of Father Pant, as if she were seeing something other than the warm, well-lit study.

'She was a woman full grown, Angela,' Father Pant said.

'She was a girl. She was always a girl. She was so young. I should have listened —.' Frau Raubal put a hand over her mouth, and shook her head again, her gaze never wavering from the spot past Father Pant.

'Should have listened?' Father Pant prompted. He was good. Fritz was grateful to be beside him.

'When she complained. She wanted to come home to Vienna.'

'But you no longer live here.'

'It is still her home.' Frau Raubal moved her hand over her eyes, and sat for a moment. Her breathing was even, her body didn't shake, she was not crying. Fritz and Father Pant sat in silence with her for quite a while. Finally, she took a deep, shuddering breath and uncovered her eyes. The intensity was back, and Fritz finally remembered where he had seen that look before: on the man who had opened the apartment door before Fritz left Munich. Angela Raubal was Adolf Hitler's sister.

Fritz swallowed, the resemblance reminding him of the questions he needed to ask. 'Forgive me, Frau Raubal, but I need to know if you think someone had reason to hurt your daughter.'

She shook her head.

'What about as a way to get to your brother?'

Her eyes went flat. It was a startling change. One moment she had blazing intensity, the next it looked as if she had left her body.

'My daughter is dead. Tomorrow we bury her. That will be the end of it. I have nothing more to say.' She stood, adjusted her skirts, and looked at Fritz. The sorrow she carried bowed her shoulders and lined her rounded face. 'Nothing we can do will change the past.'

★

'She didn't care how her daughter died?' the girl asks, interrupting him.

Fritz gazes at her. She is American. She is young. For all her studies, she does not understand, and he is not sure he can explain it to her. Angela Raubal was ten years older than Fritz. Her generation, even more than his, had lost hope of doing much more than surviving. The whys and hows were not important because whys and hows did not change things. Once an event happened, it happened, and a person had to move forward or not move at all.

'She cared,' he says. Of that, he is certain. 'She just knew she could not change it. She knew that the door to the past was closed and should remain so. I should have known that as well.'

FIFTEEN

The morning of the funeral dawned cold. September in Vienna was not as pleasant as September in Munich. Or perhaps the events of the last few days had prejudiced him. Perhaps he would feel differently about Vienna if he had come for the opera instead of investigating a murder.

Fritz arrived at the cemetery late. The service was to be performed over the grave site. All who attended would be easy to view from afar for a few moments. Now that he knew he had a murder investigation on his hands, he wanted to make certain that he had all the advantages. He did not want to be surprised by any attendees at the funeral.

The wind had picked up as he crossed the dirt path that led to the grave site. Father Pant had indicated the new area of the cemetery the day before. He had also shown Fritz the half-dug grave site outside the consecrated ground where Geli was originally going to be placed at rest. Fritz followed the new path. Geli had, at the very least, received a dignity in death.

Only a handful of people stood on the brown lawn, all dressed in black. He recognised Father Pant first, both from his robes and from his height. The ceremony hadn't started yet. Father Pant was talking with Angela Raubal. A broad shouldered young man stood beside her. From the resemblance, he was her son. Beside him was a young woman whom, Fritz first thought, was Geli in the flesh. A few couples were scattered among the mourners, and one Brownshirt, who stood some distance back. He must have been the man Father Pant alluded to the day before, the man who had threatened Dr Zerht. The man whom, Fritz suspected, Frau Winter had almost mentioned in her story about the removal of Geli's body.

Her uncle was not there, nor was any member of his household.

Fritz stuck his hands in the pocket of his overcoat, and joined the group. No one looked at him, and he did not scan the faces as a detective normally would. Instead, he focused on the coffin. This was different than the one he had seen the day before, an expensive zinc-lined model designed to preserve the body. Someone had spent a great deal of money on the arrangements, and judging from Angela Raubal's clothing, it had not been her.

Fritz stood so that he could see the SA man and Angela out of the corner of his eye. Angela's children flanked her, tears running down the young woman's face. Angela Raubal stared at the coffin, that far away look again in her eyes, but she did not cry. She appeared older than she had the day before, as if age had descended on her in the night. Her son held her hand, his face so still it could have been made of stone.

98

Father Pant took his place at the head of the mourners and, in a voice that carried over the wind, gave Geli a traditional burial. He did not use any portion of the ceremony to speak of her or her nature, nor did he discuss her death. Once, he glanced at the Brownshirt, as if wishing him away.

The SA man's stance did not change during the entire ceremony. He stood with his hands clasped behind his back, his legs spread. His boots were shiny black, and his uniform crisp. He had an oddly compelling face that Fritz felt he had seen before: it was square, with an overhanging forehead, and dark shining eyes. His gaze lingered on Fritz twice, no more and no less than it did on the others.

While Father Pant's voice rose to cover the wind, Fritz fretted about his next move. He needed to speak to the Brownshirt, but he also knew that if he did, his knowledge of the murder would become apparent. Finally, he decided to use a halfway measure. He would speak to the man, but wait until they returned to Munich before revealing his identity. It would buy him time.

Finally, Father Pant said a blessing, and when he was through, Angela Raubal knelt and kissed her daughter's coffin. Her hand lingered on the wood, her head remained bowed for a long moment. It was the only affection Fritz had seen her display toward her dead child, and because it was so unexpected, it caught in his throat. Then she stood, and the funeral was officially over.

The family would stay, and Fritz needed to speak with them, but first he had to talk with the Brownshirt. The SA man had not moved. He too watched the family as if he were waiting to speak to them. Fritz walked over to him.

The SA man watched him come, remaining in his alert posture. Fritz braced himself. He had come too close to SA before. They had a tendency toward unnecessary violence. That this man was alone didn't make him any less dangerous.

Fritz, however, was in fine physical condition. The best fighter in his unit, perhaps the best in all of Munich. He had nothing to fear from an SA man, at least, not alone.

'Hello.' Fritz stopped next to the SA man as if he were there only to make conversation. 'Such an unexpected tragedy.'

'Tragedies are always unexpected.' The SA man's voice was soft, and he spoke with a pronounced Bavarian accent.

'I understand you came from Munich with the poor girl.'

'And you followed us, Detective Inspector.'

A flush heated Fritz's cheeks and throat. He was still not used to being recognised, even though he was perhaps the most famous police officer in Bavaria. Had the Chief Inspector thought of that when he assigned Fritz to this case?

'I am at a disadvantage,' Fritz said, keeping his own tone even. 'I understand you are associated with Herr Hitler, but I do not know how.'

'My name is Hess,' the Brownshirt said, and Fritz started. It took a moment for him to orient himself. Hess, Rudolph Hess, was not a member of the SA, even though he was wearing their uniform. He was known in Munich police circles as Adolf Hitler's shadow, a man who was Secretary of the NSDAP, a man who was considered the source of the party's unusual funding. A man who was often present when something had gone awry in Hitler's life.

It had been smart of him to wear an SA uniform after discovering Geli's body. It gave him a level of protection the average German did not have. People who viewed it thought, as Fritz had, that Hess would be violently unpredictable. Anything he said in his soft voice would have three times the weight of another man.

'I had thought to see Herr Hitler here,' Fritz said.

'His political beliefs keep him out of Austria,' Hess said. 'He sent me to make certain Geli was well cared for.'

'Surely the Austrian government would make an exception for a family death.'

'One would think so.' Hess had not shifted his position during the discussion. His absolute stillness made Fritz nervous.

'Did you know Geli well?'

Hess finally moved. He turned his head so that he was looking directly at Fritz. Hess's eyes sparkled with intelligence, his lips were curled in a slight smile. 'Is this an interrogation, Inspector?'

'Should it be?' Fritz asked.

'The poor child died by her own hand. The Kripo should leave it at that.'

'The Kripo always gathers information on unusual deaths.'

'Even in closed cases?' Hess asked.

'The file must be complete,' Fritz said.

At that, Hess did smile. The expression was warm, too

warm in this cemetery on such a cold and dismal morning. 'I had heard that you concentrated on detail.'

'The press will want answers on this. You know that. The Kripo has to have something to tell them.'

'The Minister of Justice gave you something to say.' Hess swivelled his head enough to watch the other mourners.

'But with no evidence to back it up.'

'And you expected to find that evidence in Vienna? I did not know that the arm of the Munich Kripo was this long.'

'It would be easier if you talked with me,' Fritz said. The wind ruffled the hair on the back of his neck. He wished he had worn a hat.

'Easier for whom, Inspector?'

'Easier for all of us,' Fritz said. 'When you play verbal games with me, it leads me to believe you have something to hide.'

Hess unclasped his hands and brought his feet together in a crisp, military manner. 'I have nothing to hide, Inspector. I was merely surprised that the Kripo is interested in a suicide.'

Geli's brother had his arm around her sister. The young woman was sobbing. Frau Raubal was speaking to Father Pant. The wind carried their words away from Fritz.

'So, did you know Geli?' Fritz asked.

Hess sighed. 'We all knew Geli. She accompanied Hitler on all social occasions.'

'How about privately?'

He shrugged. 'My wife knew her better. Hitler was protective of Geli. He preferred her to have the company of women.'

102

'He was more than her uncle, then.'

Hess pinned Fritz with a sharp gaze. 'He was her half-uncle. Angela Raubal is his half-sister. It is a permissible relationship.'

The defensiveness made Fritz take note. Here was an issue even the party found sensitive. 'How serious was Hitler about her?'

'He loved her.' Hess spoke simply.

'Was he planning to marry her?'

Hess glanced at the mourners before speaking. 'He has been concentrating on his political career. He was going to announce his presidential campaign this weekend.'

'In Hamburg?'

'In Hamburg, yes.'

'I saw him in Munich late Saturday afternoon. How did he return from Hamburg so quickly?'

'He drove to Nuremberg on Friday. We managed to locate him there before he went farther north.'

'We?'

Hess clasped his arms behind his back again. It appeared to be a nervous gesture. 'I meant, I managed to locate him. I am used to speaking for the party.'

'And what does the party say on this?'

Hess tilted his head as he looked at Fritz. 'The party says this is a lamentable tragedy. The girl was obviously unstable. It was only a matter of time.'

'Really?' Fritz said. 'The party does not think it odd that their presidential candidate had an affair with an unstable woman who was half his age and a relative as well?'

'The party understood Hitler's relationship with Geli.

Your reaction is precisely the one we wanted to avoid when the body was discovered on Saturday.'

'What else were you trying to avoid?'

Hess tilted his head slightly. 'I do not understand.'

'You were trying to avoid scandal caused by a suicide.'

'Yes.'

'Of an unstable girl related to Herr Hitler, an unstable girl he was in love with.'

'Yes.'

'And what else?'

'Need there be anything else, Detective Inspector?'

Fritz let the words hang in the grey morning air. One of the couples was speaking to Frau Raubal, shaking her hand, the man turning his collar to guard his neck from the damp.

Finally, Fritz said, 'Who broke her nose?'

Hess's chin went up. Soldier position. 'I beg your pardon.'

'Geli. She is covered with bruises, and her nose is broken. Who did that?'

'I assume it happened when she fell.'

'Some of the bruises are old, fading.'

Hess was watching the mourners leave. He would not look at Fritz. 'I told you, she was an unstable girl.'

'An unstable girl who shoots herself in the chest, and then falls *forward,* thus breaking her nose. Do you expect me to believe this, Herr Hess?'

Hess shifted so that his feet were apart again, his entire body on guard. In the tight SA uniform, he projected a considerable threat. Fritz was as large, and in better shape. He braced himself as well.

104

'I expect you to believe the Minister of Justice,' Hess said.

'I am not as easily bought,' Fritz said.

'You malign Franz Gürtner.'

'You cannot malign a man who bases his judicial opinion on money, cronyism, and a phone call from an associate. Such a man maligns himself.'

'The matter is closed, Inspector.'

'A woman has been murdered, Herr Hess, in the home of the man you are backing for President. Have you no fear that her attacker will return for Hitler? Or do you know that Hitler was never a target?'

Hess's eyes narrowed. 'Inspector, we are not on German soil here.'

Fritz straightened. Finally, they had come to the violence he expected. Or the intimation of violence.

'And since we are not,' Hess said, noting Fritz's change in posture, 'I shall speak freely and then deny anything I have said if others ask.'

Fritz felt a chill run down his back.

'Geli's death has come at an opportune time for Herr Hitler's enemies, and in the perfect location.'

'Are you saying she was murdered?'

'If she were – and I am not saying that she was – the time and place of her death would have created problems for Herr Hitler.'

'Who would need to set him up?' Fritz asked.

Hess's smile was small, cold. 'Talk with Gregor Strasser. Ask what would happen to him if Herr Hitler were no longer leading the party.'

'You tell me,' Fritz said.

Hess lowered his chin, the look both condescending and cold. 'You really should follow politics more, Detective Inspector.'

He would. He would follow the lead. It was more than he expected from Hess. 'If she were murdered by one of Hitler's enemies, isn't it better to reveal that?'

'Come now, Inspector. Not even you are so naïve. This is our year. We may never get another chance. Better to close the case than to run a campaign during an on-going police investigation.'

'Better to let a murderer go, to let a threat to Hitler continue than to risk a few weeks bad publicity.'

This time, Hess's smile was broad. He brought his head forward once, not fast enough to be a nod, not slow enough to be anything else. 'You are as quick as they say.' The tone was mocking.

'Perhaps not,' Fritz said. 'I revel in difficult cases.'

Hess crossed his arms over his broad chest. 'Geli Raubal committed suicide. That is a fact you should remember, Inspector.'

Fritz clenched his fists, energy running through his arms. He hated the smugness on Hess's square face. 'Are you threatening me?'

'I have no need to, Inspector,' Hess said. 'You threaten yourself. Now, if you'll excuse me, I am to speak to the family.'

He walked away, his stride long and athletic. Fritz watched him go. Fritz had known the NSDAP since its inception years before. He had not thought of the party as particularly powerful. Perhaps he would have to rethink his impressions.

Hess continued his walk to the open grave. Fritz watched him mingle with the Raubal family. They greeted him like an old friend which, in truth, he probably was.

★

'Why didn't you speak with the family?' the girl says.

'You get ahead of me,' Fritz replies. He shifts in his chair. The spring is digging into his back. 'I spoke to them after Hess left. They did not know anything of Geli's life in Munich. The sister, Friedl, obviously looked up to Geli, and envied her abilities with men. The brother was protective, but dismissive. He had not spent much time with her since she was a girl. And he did say that she had always been Hitler's favourite, even as a child.'

'And what about her mother?' the girl asks.

Fritz takes a cigarette from his pack, taps the end on the table, and then puts the cigarette in his mouth. 'She said nothing.'

'This didn't bother you?'

'Of course it bothered me,' Fritz says, 'but not in the way you think. Angela Raubal was the one who let her daughter live in Munich without supervision. She had to have known Hitler's feeling for Geli. She had to have known the dangerous people her brother associated with. She had to have known that her daughter was flighty and flirtatious, and still she allowed Geli to live away from her.'

'Geli was a grown woman, for all you call her a girl.'

'Yes, but it was customary in good Catholic families to keep the unmarried daughters at home.'

'Even after 1923?'

So the American does have some inkling of history. Fritz picks up his lighter, flicks the end, and watches the butane flame flare. He

107

touches the flame to the cigarette and inhales, enjoying the cool burn as it travels down his throat into his chest. 'Especially after 1923,' he says.

SIXTEEN

Fritz was exhausted when he arrived at his own apartment. The scarred door, with its twisted 'No 3', never looked so inviting. He shifted the duffel over his shoulder, and crouched to pick up the morning's *Münchner Post* . He was not too tired to note the headline, *A Mysterious Affair: Hitler's Niece Commits Suicide,* nor to realise its implications for him. He tucked the paper under his arm and let himself inside, no longer relieved to be home.

On the trip back he had replayed the conversation with Hess over and over again. Fritz hadn't wanted Geli's death to be murder. He had wanted a suicide, something he could confirm. Now, not only did he have to examine Hitler's household, he had to examine the NSDAP, something which made him decidedly uneasy.

He pressed the button on the wall switch, turning on the overhead light. His apartment was small – a single room with a shared bath in the hall – but neat. The dishes from his breakfast on Saturday morning dried in the rack beside the small sink, the apartment's only luxury. His cot rested beneath the window, the frayed army blanket that he had somehow managed to keep through all the tribulations after the war was folded carefully on top of the crisp white sheets. A small shelf of books covered the wall beside the wobbly wooden table, and the closet door was open, revealing his only vice, a passion for nice clothing. He had lost his faith in currency in the Great Inflation, but could not bring himself to part with his money. Instead, he invested it in gold when he could, and undeveloped land north of Munich. He would never put his faith in paper again.

He set his duffel inside the closet, then sat on the couch, sinking into the thick cushions. With the flick of a switch he turned on the lamp on the end-table he bought with his first Kripo paycheck. It had cigarette burns now, and a coffee stain that would not come out, but he was still proud of it. The end table was a symbol of his ability to survive, no matter what the world threw at him. He had to remember that, throughout this case.

Carefully, he unfolded the *Post* and read the article:

Regarding this mysterious affair, informed sources tell us that on Friday, September 18, Herr Hitler and his niece had yet another fierce quarrel. What was the cause? Geli, a vivacious twenty-three year-old music student, wanted to go to Vienna, where she intended to become engaged....

Engaged? No one had mentioned that. And the only unattached young man at the funeral was Geli's brother, Leo. How odd that a man who would be planning to marry the girl would not show up to honour her in death.

...Hitler was decidedly against this. That is why they were

quarrelling repeatedly. After a fierce row, Hitler left his
apartment on Prinzregentenplaz.

Frau Reichert had said they quarrelled, and Frau Winter
had implied it. Frau Reichert had said that Geli wanted to
go to Vienna, which was why they fought, but Frau Winter
said Geli had discovered a letter from another woman in
Hitler's pocket, and the jealousy had driven Geli to suicide.
A young woman about to marry another man did not kill
herself with jealousy over the man she was leaving.

On Saturday, September 19, it became known that Geli had
been found shot in the apartment with Hitler's gun in her
hand. The nose bone of the deceased was shattered and the
corpse evidenced other serious injuries. From a letter to a
girlfriend living in Vienna, it appeared that Geli intended to
go to Vienna…

Fritz stared at the paragraph. He had had to go to Vienna
himself to get that information, yet the *Post* had it right
here. The *Post* was known for its anti-Nazi sympathies. They
had to have had a source in NSDAP headquarters, the
Brown House. They certainly didn't get the information
from the women, and the body left Munich too quickly. Or
had it? He had never checked what train Hess took, nor its
arrival time.

He made mental note of that, then continued reading.

The men at the Brown House then deliberated over what
should be announced as the cause of the suicide. They agreed
to give the reason for Geli's death as 'unsatisfied artistic

111

achievement'. They also discussed the question of who, if something were to happen, should be Hitler's successor. Gregor Strasser was named...

★

'A successor?' the girl says. 'They chose a successor to Hitler? Is this true?'

Fritz raises his chin, much as Hess had done at the funeral. Old soldiers had the same reflexes. 'Everything I tell you is true,' he says.

'But the papers, even now not everything they print is true.'

'This was.'

'A successor. So that's why Hess told you about Strasser, because Strasser was the one with something to gain.' She shakes her head, then breathes out, almost a sigh. 'Imagine it. A world without Hitler.'

He gazes at her. The dreamy look on her face, so familiar –

He shakes himself, and forces himself to continue.

★

The *Post* did have a source in the Brown House. There would be no way they would have known this information other-wise. Damn the Chief Inspector. Fritz needed more men. He had needed more men on Saturday. He might have got to Max Amann and Franz Xavier Schwarz before they were able to make up a complete story. He might have been able to break the coalition.

But now he was working behind them, and they knew it. This article showed him that he could not rest. He had to resolve this case quickly. First, he would get Henrich Felke's help. Then he would cover as much ground as he could. Someone had murdered Geli Raubal, and the murder was considered important enough by one of Germany's political parties to instigate a cover-up. They smuggled the body out of the country and then made up a story to hide the facts of her death. The NSDAP was frightened – and with reason.

One of their members might have killed Geli Raubal.

He had to find out who had done so – and soon.

SEVENTEEN

He pauses there and pulls his cigar box from under his chair. He opens it and removes the wrapped newspaper clippings from the bottom. The newsprint is yellow and fragile. He must unfold the articles carefully before handing them, one by one, to the girl.

She studies them as if she will be quizzed on them. Absently, she reaches beside her and shuts off the tape. Then she grabs her notepad and writes down the dates.

He has quoted to her the only article he remembers, and he remembers it because it shocked him. The other articles, which he gathered later, are more explicit, given to wild speculations. Each paper had its own idea of what happened. Some were lurid accounts of assassins who arrived planning to kill Hitler, and getting Geli instead. Others speculated that Hitler had shot the girl himself. Still others claimed that Geli was pregnant by a Jew and had to be killed to protect Hitler. She was alternately beautiful in death, beaten to unrecognisability, shot through the head or the heart, and wearing nothing, or a brown robe, or a blue nightgown.

The most accurate report was the one he read first, and the one he concentrated on. But the girl reads them all, that small frown furrowing her brow. Finally, she looks at him and hands him a *brittle clipping. It too is from the* Münchner Post, *although he has a matching one that first appeared in the* Völkischer Beobachter. *It is a letter, signed by Adolf Hitler, which reads:*

1) It is not true that I was having fights again and again with my niece Geli Raubal and that we had a substantial quarrel on Friday or any time before that.

2) It is not true that I was decidedly against her going to Vienna. I was never against her planned trip to Vienna.

3) It is not true she was going to get engaged in Vienna or that I was against the engagement. It is true that my niece was tormented with worry that she was not yet fit for her public appearance. She wanted to go to Vienna to have her voice checked once again by a voice teacher.

4) It is not true that I left my apartment on September 18 after a fierce row. There was no row, no excitement, when I left my apartment on that day.

'It is so defensive,' the girl says.

'Yes.' Fritz stares at the clipping. To this day he is not certain if Hitler actually wrote the document, if one of his cronies did, or if one of his enemies did to discredit him. The statement's very existence shows the divisions within the NSDAP.

She hands the rest of the clippings back to him, and stands. 'I want to make you lunch,' she says. 'An American lunch.'

For the first time, he notices that she left one bag on the counter when she brought in breakfast. When she had entered, he had been thinking of his dream, of Geli's brutalised body, and had not watched the girl very closely.

116

'Do you miss your American food?' he asks.

'A little,' she says. 'The meals are so heavy here. I feel as if I have gained eighty pounds.'

She is trim, almost too thin. German women are not that thin. Such thinness, here, is a sign of poverty – at least to men like him. Fat is a sign that a man can afford to feed his family, and feed them well. But Americans have never suffered. They do not understand these matters and try to maintain an unnatural look at all times.

She goes into the kitchen and begins to unload items from the bag. He recognises many of them as canned goods from the American-style supermarket built near the autobahn.

'Don't worry,' she says. 'It looks like a lot, but it won't take very long.'

'That's fine.' He needs to rest anyway. His throat is dry, has been dry and sore for days. He is not used to talking to anyone. He goes through his days wandering through the English Garden, reading books he buys – often American now – and going to movies of all kinds. When he goes to a beer hall, he speaks to the others at the tables, but he is usually alone. The Chief Inspector died last year of a liver ailment, and Henrich moved to Nuremberg, too sick to care for himself, an invalid in the hands of a daughter he barely knew. Fritz called him once or twice, but to hear hearty Henrich filled with such despair depressed him even farther. Perhaps because they had nothing when they were young, the men of his generation did not believe what they had when they were old. After retirement, life became a simple waiting game, waiting for death, for more tragedy to strike.

Fritz's life has contracted, even though he has not worked for decades. His resurgent celebrity brought some promotional appearances, a false camaraderie among the fashionable in Munich and West Berlin, a sense of purpose he had lacked. But that faded, and with it his interest in the world around him. The interest on his money feeds and clothes him, but he has no one to leave the money to. No one will remember Fritz the man after the Fritz the famous Kripo officer is completely and officially dead.

The girl is searching through cupboards in his kitchen, finally removing thin soup bowls he barely remembers he owns. Then she takes his metal ladle and two spoons, and ladles liquid from the stewpot. His stomach growls. He has not been watching her cook. He hadn't realised how hungry he was.

Finally she brings him a bowl filled with carrots, onions, broccoli, green beans, tomatoes and macaroni in a thick tomato broth. No meat, although he searches for it as he spoons his first bite. Only beans and macaroni. A poor man's dinner. Still, he smiles and thanks her, and then tastes, surprised at the flavourings she has used.

She watches him like an expectant mother – no one has cared about what he has eaten for decades. He smiles and nods, approving, although he feels vaguely odd about the absent meat. The soup eases his dry, sore throat, and restores him. He hopes she will leave it on the burner all afternoon so that he may refill his bowl whenever his voice gets tired.

She eats her own meal at the table, away from her recorder, staring at his pictures. So far, she has not asked him about them, but it will only be a matter of time. When she does, he is not certain how much he will tell her.

He feels as if he has told her too much already.

EIGHTEEN

He bathed and changed clothes before leaving again, buying a cup of coffee from a late-night restaurant on his way to Prinzregentenplaz. The coffee revived him enough to make him alert, but not enough to wipe the gritty feeling from his eyes. Despite his best intentions, he would have to get some sleep. He would do no one any good if he could not think clearly.

He had made a mental list. He still had one eyewitness he hadn't spoken to. After he spoke with the old woman, Frau Dachs, he would talk with Gregor Strasser, other members of the NSDAP, and Hitler himself.

First, Fritz went to Prinzregentenplaz. The old woman would have to be in so late at night. He would speak to her and get the letter. Then he would get some much needed rest.

Lights were on in the stone apartment building, but only one light burned on the second floor. He hoped it was Hitler's.

Nothing had changed inside as Fritz climbed the stairs to the second floor. He almost expected to see reporters clamouring for a story, Brownshirts holding them away. But the entry and hall were eerily silent.

It took a long time for anyone to respond to his knock. He heard a vague rustling behind the door before it was pulled open and he made a mental note: the building was so silent at night that the smallest sounds, covered in the daytime by ambient noise, were made audible. The door opened slowly. Frau Reichert stood before him, holding a nightdress closed at her throat.

'Forgive me for disturbing you, Frau Reichert,' he said, 'but I need to speak with your mother.'

Frau Reichert's eyes were large on her face. She had deep shadows beneath them and her skin was pale. If anything, she looked even more haggard than she had on Saturday.

'I am sorry, Detective Inspector,' she said softly. 'She does not want visitors.'

'It's important that I speak with her.'

'She is an old woman. It is nearly midnight. She is already asleep.'

'Wake her, please.'

Frau Reichert shook her head. 'I cannot.'

'Then let me.'

'I am not to let anyone inside,' she said. She glanced over her shoulder.

Fritz resisted the urge to push open the door. 'Who is behind you?'

'No one,' Frau Reichert whispered.

'You are alone here? What about Frau Winter?'

'She has gone home.'

'And what of Herr Hitler?'

'He is not in.'

'When do you expect him back?'

'He is out of town.'

'Has he gone back to Hamburg, then?'

She shook her head, then glanced over her shoulder again. 'I do not know where he is.'

'Frau Reichert, it is important that I speak to him.'

'I know,' she said. 'But he is not here.'

'Where is Herr Hitler, Frau Reichert?'

'I do not know!' she cried. 'Please, leave us be. Please.'

She was about to close the door when Fritz put his hand on it.

'What are you so afraid of?' His voice was soft, cajoling. 'The Kripo can help you.'

'The Kripo helps no one,' she said. 'Please, Inspector. It is not good to keep coming here.'

'Why not, Frau Reichert? Will something happen to me?'

She shook her head, her knuckles white as her grip on her nightdress tightened. 'It is just not good. Enough has happened already.'

'Frau Reichert,' Fritz said, keeping his voice soft, 'why didn't Herr Hitler go to Geli's funeral?'

'He could not,' she said. 'He could not. Her death has destroyed him.'

'Destroyed him? Or his career?'

She glanced over her shoulder again. 'Please leave, Inspector. You can learn nothing more here.'

Except the identity of the other person behind the door. He pushed just enough to force the door past Frau Reichert's sturdy body. She was alone in the dark entry hall.

121

'Who were you looking at, Frau Reichert?'

'No one,' she said. 'I just do not like to be alone here.'

'But you said your mother is with you.'

'She is asleep, and I would like to be too. Frau Winter will be here in the morning. She may know where Herr Hitler is. Please, Inspector, I cannot help you.'

The tears welled in her eyes. She looked very frail, standing alone in the entryway, the unwilling guardian of a thousand secrets.

'I'm sorry,' he said. 'Please tell your mother and Frau Winter that I will see them tomorrow.'

'Yes, sir,' Frau Reichert said, and gently, ever so gently, closed the door.

Fritz stood before it, head bowed, for a long time. The Chief Inspector had assigned him a difficult task and then made it impossible. Even if he did gather enough evidence on the murder, what then? The Minister of Justice had already ruled on it. The case was closed.

Finally, Fritz sighed and went down the stairs. He too would get sleep. He could do nothing else until morning.

*

He stops, wipes his face. He is sweating even though the room is cool. The next part he has to tell her makes him uncomfortable. He had not thought of it at first. But now, now that he has come to this part of his tale, he finds that he cannot speak. The soup, which he is grateful for, has suddenly become a barrier between them. She has done something domestic, something female. She has cared for him. And it is not until this moment that he realises she is of a gentler breed. She is young enough to be his granddaughter. She has a purity in her face.

122

Like Gisela once did.

'Are you all right?' she asks.

'I think I will have more soup,' he says, to fortify himself. He will have to tell her. He cannot stop here. The tale is begun. He must finish it. Not for her, but for himself.

He pushes himself out of the chair, grabs his bowl, and ladles out more. She has made enough to feed ten men. As if her meagre efforts will aid him. He can take care of himself. He always has.

'If you don't mind,' she says as he sits back down, 'I would like to leave a bit early this afternoon. I would like to see if I can get Photostats of those clips.'

He nods. He does not know how much more he can say today. It has been difficult for him so far, and it will only get more difficult.

'Would you like to leave now?' he asks.

'No.' She puts a new cassette in the recorder. 'I think we have another hour or two.'

'Well, then,' he says, stirring the vegetables with his spoon. 'Let's make the most of it.'

NINETEEN

The caffeine had worn off by the time he reached his apartment. He could feel the stress of the long drive in his shoulders, the tension of the case in his back. He would have to set an alarm so that he could wake just after dawn, otherwise he would sleep the entire morning away.

He unlocked his apartment door, and the slap of paper against wood startled him. He looked down to see a large envelope – the kind the Kripo used for inter-office correspondence – lying across the threshold. He kicked the envelope inside, then looked to either side. He appeared to be alone in the hallway. With one swift movement he slipped inside the apartment, closed the door, and locked it.

The lights were still on and the paper was spread over his couch, just as he had left it. Nothing else was out of place. He slid his hand inside his sleeve, grabbed the envelope, took it to the table and sat, studying it.

The envelope was new, without markings, a dull brown identifying it as foreign – probably British. The glued end was sealed. For a moment he toyed with waiting until morning to open it, but it would serve no purpose. He was conducting this investigation on his own, outside of the precinct, and he knew the procedures as well as any of them. He had helped develop those procedures.

He set the envelope on the table and went to his small chest of drawers, removing his thinnest pair of gloves. He slipped them on, the wool warming his already hot skin. Then he used the tip of his pocket knife to carefully slit the bottom of the envelope. He did not want to interfere with the upper seal, in case anything was caught in it.

He set the knife down, slipped his fingers inside the envelope, and pulled out six pieces of rag paper. They curled slightly when removed. He spread them out on the table and stared.

They were watercolours of a nude woman. In the first, she was standing Grecian style, a white robe held in her right hand flowed over her legs, as if she had just revealed her nakedness to someone. She was looking down, her expression sad. In the second, she reclined on a lounge, one leg bent at the knee, the other straight. Again, she was looking away from the artist.

All of the paintings were imitations of classic nudes, only without the delicate draping. The woman's pubic hair showed in all of the paintings, her ski-jump breasts with their brown nipples a prominent feature. Only the sixth was done in a different style. In that painting, the woman was on her back, lying on rumpled sheets, one arm flung above her head, the other at her side. Her eyes were closed, her mouth open. Her legs were spread, and the artist spent loving time and detail on the pubic area. In fact, the woman's pubis was the centre of the painting. The rest of the details flowed from there.

The artist was marginally talented with an ability to mimic life. He appeared to have trouble with limbs. In all of the paintings, the woman's arms were too long, and in the last, her legs had too much flesh between the thigh and knee. But he was good enough to make his subject recognisable.

Geli, without the bruises or the broken nose. Fritz recognised her more from the light dusting of pubic hair than from her facial features. This was the body he had seen, bloodless and lifeless in Vienna.

The paintings had been done by the same artist who had executed the watercolours in Hitler's flat. The same use of colour, the same mistakes, were evident. Fritz thumbed through the watercolours looking for an artist's signature. Most of them did not have signatures, but the one of the woman reclining on the lounge did. In the same mixed black-brown that filled in the legs of the lounge, the artist had written his name. The first name was almost unreadable – at first Fritz thought it said 'by' instead of a name at all – but the last name was clear. *Hitler.* A tiny, cramped signature that ran downhill. Fritz wondered what the graphologists would make of that. Then he was able to make out the loosely formed 'A' in Adolf, and the long lower-case 'f' with the bar on its tail.

Fritz put a gloved hand on his forehead. Someone had wanted him to have this. More information about the case, information someone didn't want to tell him directly.

*****

'Why didn't they take the paintings to the press?' the girl asks. 'They would have discredited Hitler immediately.'

Fritz shakes his head. 'The papers were as easily discredited. We did not have the faith you Americans have in your media. We knew they could be bought and often were. No, I got the paintings because I was the only man in a position to do anything with them.'

*****

Now he wished he had searched the hallway more carefully. Perhaps he would have found the person who had left the paintings. Although he doubted it. This was not the kind of information a man kept on a political figure without good reason.

*****

How did you know it was a man?' the girl asks.

'I didn't,' he says.

*****

This case made his skin crawl. He couldn't be certain of anything. Geli's closeness to Hitler, and his presence as leader of the NSDAP made even the simplest things suspect. Fritz didn't know if someone had left these paintings with him to discredit Hitler the candidate, or to point the finger of blame at Hitler the murderer. Or, if the paintings were meant as a diversion to cast suspicion on a man who was innocent, a man who had nothing to do with Geli's death. Hitler claimed to have been out of town. If he was, then this murder of his niece was a great way to derail a candidacy that hadn't yet started, just as Hess had implied.

Fritz gathered up the paintings. He paused as he did so

and stared at Geli's face. In each she was looking away from the artist. In the last her eyes were closed, her face expressionless. Fritz had seen such paintings before. Usually the woman tried to seduce, her lips pouty, her eyes open, her expression flirtatious. Geli made no attempt here, and Hitler made no attempt to portray her in that manner. If anything, her expression in the other paintings was sad.

He put them in a different order, with the signed one first. An artist signed his work when he expected others to view it. Hitler had signed the paintings in the flat. Fritz would wager the remaining five paintings, Hitler had done for himself.

Hitler couldn't have left them on Fritz's doorstep. The last thing Hitler would have wanted would be to have the paintings in the hand of the Kripo. So someone else had to have had them in the first place. Someone with access to the apartment, perhaps, or access to Hitler. Or Geli.

Fritz took a folder off his shelf and put the drawings in it. He would do the fingerprinting on them himself. He didn't know anyone else he could trust. He didn't want knowledge of the paintings getting out until he knew for certain who had killed Geli Raubal.

But the envelope might carry a wealth of information. And the envelope he would take to the precinct.

*

'Didn't you think it dangerous to leave the paintings in your home?' The girl is more animated than he has seen her. She usually listens to him, and questions little. But the paintings disturb her in a way he can't completely identify.

'It was more dangerous to have them at the precinct,' he says. 'At

that time, policemen were encouraged to join political parties as long as their affiliation did not interfere with their work. Both the Communists and the Nazis – mostly the Communists – used their positions to gain information that would help their political parties. I was afraid someone would take the paintings and use them in a way I did not intend.'

'But what could you do with them?'

'Inquire about them. Use them to shock at the right moment. I was hoping to present them to Hitler and gauge his reaction.'

'Hoping?' she asks.

He smiles. 'You get ahead of me.'

'You sound as if you did not show him the paintings.'

He picks up the pack of matches and taps them next to the half-full soup bowl. 'It bothers you that you know nothing about this case, doesn't it? You want to know the ending so that you know how clever I was in my work.'

She stops the tape. 'I feel as if I am at your mercy. I have to take your opinion as fact.'

'You don't have to. You can research this. I am sure the Münchner Post *has record of this case.'*

'But you said it was an anti-Nazi newspaper.'

'So I did.' He cups the matches in his right hand. 'But you have never asked me if I were anti-Nazi at that time.'

'I don't have to,' she says. 'You seem to have been afraid of them.'

'Ach.' He has not wanted to give her that impression. In those days, he was afraid of everyone and nothing at the same time. 'I was so strong in those days I could lift a man twice my size without straining my back. I ran faster than any other man in Kripo, and I was often sent to riot patrol because I could use a truncheon better

130

than any of my colleagues. I could defend myself from any physical threat, although I never wanted to.'

'So you did not see them as a physical threat.'

He reaches for a cigarette. The pack is empty. He tosses it aside, grabs another pack, and unwraps the cellophane. 'I saw them as a measure of the craziness that we had allowed into Germany.' He does not look at her as he says that. He has never really said that to anyone before.

'Craziness?' she says.

'You would not understand. You and your peaceful, successful country.' His fingers are too thick to grip the slim end of the gold foil covering the cigarette pack. When he is alone, he breaks the pack open with his teeth. He cannot do so now. He sets the pack down.

'I understand,' she says. 'Hitler was your craziness.'

'No.' He clenches a fist, wondering how to explain everything to her. Her lack of history, her people's continual search for the easy answer, makes this harder than it needs to be. He takes a deep breath.

'We came back from the war, all of us, different in some way. A man cannot see –' his voice cracks. He clears his throat, does not look at her, picks up the pack again '– he cannot see his best friend explode into tiny fragments beside him and ever be the same again.'

'My grandfather saw such things. He never wanted to talk about war.'

'Your grandfather –' Fritz shakes the pack at her. 'Your grandfather did not come home to a defeated country, remodelled after the countries that defeated it. He did not come home to starvation, and poverty, and disease –'

He can still see Gisela, in the last month of her failed pregnancy, her body so thin that the bones in her neck are prominent. She

131

screeches at him, and the baby cries, little Wilhelm, a tiny reedy sound, screeches that there is not enough food and what is he doing anyway? Nothing. Nothing to help them. Nothing to save their three lives. All she does is live for the new child. The new child, born dead one afternoon in a gout of blood.

'– and then he cannot get a job, and his family starves, and the money he has, the things he has, are worth less and less, until he is begging on the street. Your grandfather did not come home to that.' Fritz puts the cigarette pack in his teeth and bites off the end, pulling out a cigarette like the prize in a raffle.

'No, he did not,' the girl says. 'But you did.'

'I did, and millions of other men. Millions, my girl. Do you know what the First World War did to us? It killed or maimed seven million men, seven million Germans. That does not count Austrians or Russians. Just Germans. And you Americans talk of that war as if you had a part in it. Only four million of your men were even engaged. And only 300,000 were casualties of that war. You have no idea what it did to us.'

'What it did to you,' she says.

He stares at her for a long moment. His cigarette has a piece of foil hanging from the end. She meets his gaze in the same measured fashion. 'That's right,' he says finally. 'You have no idea what it did to me.'

TWENTY

Fritz hated going to the Brown House. It had only been NSDAP headquarters for nine months, but in that time he had gone on many visits, sometimes with the political police as a guard, and sometimes on cases involving disputes with the Communists. The Brown House had once been Barlow Palace, and he continued to think of it that way, although to say so brought loud correction from anyone within hearing distance. The majestic view over Königsplaz belonged to a king, not to a tawdry political party whose leader's niece had just been murdered.

This part of Munich had been the home to Ludwig the First, who abdicated in 1848. Fritz had always thought of Ludwig as a much more ancient king, perhaps because the buildings he sponsored had the look of Greece to them – the long, flowing columns, the grand arches. This was a regal part of Munich, regal and cold. As a boy, Fritz had walked through it, imagining himself at the mercy of men who were greater than he was.

The Brownshirts of the NSDAP did not belong here. Misfits and beer hall brawlers, they had obtained a sort of status in the last election, gaining almost 100 seats in the Reichstag by preaching a confused message of economic hope and hatred of groups, from the Communists to the Jews. Fritz had heard many of the speeches, impassioned all of them, and part of him wanted to believe them: that if Germany were only cleansed of its foreign element, it would be great again. If Germany stood on its own legs, it would be able to provide for its citizens. But ultimately, the speakers never said anything of consequence. They did not have a program for developing their reforms; they simply knew that change had to be made.

Fritz believed in detail, and the NSDAP's denial of detail would have troubled him even if he hadn't been in the Kripo. But he was, and as a member of the police force – even though he was not often on the street – he saw the one thing that made him turn away from NSDAP altogether: the violence. If a man could not be silenced by words, he was silenced with truncheons. Dissenters were beaten, sometimes to death.

A party based on violence would lead to a government based on the same violence, a government that would not listen to any voice raised in protest.

Despite his dislike for the Brown House, he was at their door before most of the men had arrived. His day had started even earlier: he had already spoken to Henrich, who agreed to begin his assistance by getting the letter from Frau Winter. Henrich had offered to accompany Fritz to the Brown House, but Fritz felt better in such a place alone. He did not want to have to protect someone else, particularly someone he had brought along unofficially.

When Fritz arrived, the door to the Brown House was unlocked. The lower floor was empty, except for a few party clerks who had arrived for work early. Even they wore pseudo military uniforms. They did not roll up their sleeves like other clerks in other party buildings. They wore boots and saluted crisply after speaking. Fritz avoided them and slipped into the small refreshment room he knew to be on the side.

Once he had found Hitler there, on an afternoon after the SA had broken up a Communist rally. On this morning, the refreshment centre was empty except for a slender young clerk whose white shirt was buttoned tightly around his neck, and whose blond hair was cut short, military style.

'I am looking for Herr Hitler,' Fritz said.

'He is not in, sir. May I help you?' The boy's voice still broke from youth.

Fritz smiled at him, deciding in this military environ, the kindly older uncle routine would be a welcome change. 'If he is not here, I would like to see Herr Amann or Herr Schwarz.'

The boy flushed. 'I'm sorry, sir. It is a bit early for the offices to be full.'

'Is Herr Strasser in?'

The boy straightened slightly. 'I thought I saw Herr Strasser upstairs.'

Fritz let his smile broaden. 'I would love to see him, if I could.'

'I will take you upstairs,' the boy said.

But Fritz laid a hand on his arm. 'No. Just point me in the right direction. You probably have many tasks to get on with.'

'Thank you, sir, but it would be no trouble.'

'Ah,' Fritz said quietly. 'But it might, if you understand my meaning.'

The boy did. He was clearly used to secret meetings and discussions that clerks were not privy to. In clear, precise language accompanied by a flurry of hand signals, the boy gave Fritz directions to Strasser's office. Fritz thanked the boy, and went upstairs.

The Brown House still had some of the palace's former glory, but it had been lessened somehow. Even though the House was spotless, it had a tawdry air. Some of the change was the decorations: the blood flags flown during the 1923 putsch hung from the walls, the desks, and the phones (which had started ringing shortly after Fritz arrived, and never seemed to stop), and the party members themselves, who marched in as if they were part of a military regime.

When he reached the second floor, the sound of the phones grew fainter. The air was chill and smelled of leather. The ancient marble covering the floor was cloudy white, like ice on a wind-shrouded lake. Even though the large windows let in a lot of light, the glass diffused it, making it as cold as the rest of the place.

He checked in the other offices. They were empty, the doors surprisingly unlocked, although nothing sat on desktops except telephones, pen holders and calendars. Hitler's office was the largest and the most obvious. The marble floor had been covered with a reddish-brown carpet, with furniture to match. The windows overlooked

Mussolini stood against one wall, amed photographs.

de and stood before the row of nong them was one of a World War I unit, in the centre, looking thinner and tired. was a studio portrait of a beautiful woman. She black hair combed into a subtle marcel. Her eyebrows were plucked to single curved lines, and she wore only a slight tinge of make-up. A fur wrap warmed her shoulders, leaving her neck and collar bare. But those details were not the ones that made her stunning: it was her expression. Her eyes held a proud warmth, her chin was jutted forward, suggesting confidence, and her near-smile was just enough to make her appear mysterious and inviting at the same time.

It took him a moment to recognise the face. Geli. The photograph made her look older and more sophisticated than her years suggested.

But she had no cunning, like Gisela had had.

None at all.

The hair on the back of his neck prickled. He was being watched. He whirled. A man peered in the door. He was not wearing the uniform of the clerks, nor was he dressed as a Brownshirt. He wore a suit, and wire-framed glasses that enlarged his eyes. He was balding, his features soft, his mouth in a straight line. He clearly had not expected Fritz to be in Hitler's office.

'I'm looking for Gregor Strasser,' Fritz said.

The man studied him for a moment, as if Fritz had spoken

a completely foreign language. Then the man said, '○
Strasser's office is down the hall, to the right.'

'Thank you,' Fritz said, and pushed past the man. The m
did not follow him, nor did he say anything else. When Fr
finally arrived at Strasser's office, he turned, and the strange
man was gone.

Strasser's door was open as well. His office lacked the
opulence of Hitler's. The polished desk was clear, the single
window had its curtains drawn back. It did not look as if
anyone had been in the office all morning.

Fritz sighed. He didn't want to make an appointment,
didn't want his name known more than it was. But he also
knew his time was limited. He simply could not be
everywhere. He had to choose his meetings, and choose
them well.

'Who let you up here?' The voice boomed in the marble
hallway. Fritz turned. The man facing him was bowed with
middle age. His round face suggested his stout build came
from too much beer rather than too much exercise. He had
the sharp-eyed look of a man with no sense of humour.

'I was told I would find Herr Strasser here.'

The man assessed Fritz. 'You are a reporter?'

'No.'

'Then what are you to see Herr Strasser for?'

Fritz returned the stare. He was taller than the other man
and more athletic, both of which he could use to his
advantage if he had to. 'I do not routinely tell one man
another's business.'

A smile touched the other man's lips. He apparently

enjoyed jousting. 'You can tell me. I am the party treasurer. I know all the secrets.'

'I bet you do, Herr Schwarz,' Fritz said, keeping his own glee from his face. Finally someone he did need to see. 'I am Detective Inspector Stecher. I am here about Geli Raubal.'

Herr Schwarz clasped his hands behind his back. 'Such a tragedy. The poor child.'

'Yes.' Fritz took a step toward him. 'Is there a place where we can talk?'

'We're the only ones on the floor, Inspector.'

'I saw another man only a moment ago. I prefer some privacy.'

Herr Schwarz brought his chin up with unfeigned surprise. He hadn't known about the other man.

'There is my office,' he said. He led Fritz farther down the opulent hallway to an office no bigger than a walk-in closet. A goose-necked lamp was on the desk, illuminating some papers scattered on top. Files stood under the window. This looked like a place where someone worked.

Herr Schwarz pulled out a chair for Fritz, then sat behind his desk. He slid the papers in a drawer with an easy movement that appeared to be born of habit. Then he folded his hands on the empty desktop. The round pool of light from the lamp spotlighted his clasped fingers. 'How may I help you, Inspector?'

'I understand you were on site when Geli Raubal's body was discovered.'

Herr Schwarz smiled tightly. 'Not quite. Frau Reichert called me, quite upset, and I came as quickly as I could.'

'Why did she call you, Herr Schwarz?'

'Is this an official interrogation, Inspector?'

Fritz crossed his legs and leaned back in the chair. 'It's not an interrogation. It is an inquiry. We need to finish our paperwork before we can close the file.'

'The girl is dead and buried, a suicide. It would seem the file is already closed.'

Fritz smiled. 'Would that it were so easy.'

'It sounds as if the Kripo has more paperwork than Reichstag.'

'New bureaucracies only seem to create litters of paper.'

'But I thought the Bavarian government did not follow all of the policies of Berlin.'

'No,' Fritz said. 'It only follows the most inconvenient ones.'

Both men laughed, but the sound was polite – more a requirement of the kind of conversation they were having than any real enjoyment they felt.

'Well, then,' Herr Schwarz said, 'I will help you in any way I can.'

'Then tell me why Frau Reichert called you.'

Herr Schwarz unclasped his hands and pushed his chair away from his desk. 'Herr Hitler was out of town and –' again the tiny smile '– Frau Reichert is the type of woman who cannot make decisions for herself. I probably would not have come if Frau Winter had been there.'

'Frau Winter can make decisions for herself?'

Herr Schwarz raised his eyebrows. 'Have you met Frau Winter?'

'Yes.'

'Then you already know. I arrived, took one look at the poor girl, and knew we had to take some action.'

'Action, Herr Schwarz?'

'We could not leave her in such a sorry position in the Führer's apartment.'

Führer. Leader. Fritz had heard the word used in reference to Hitler before but had not thought about it until that moment. He had assumed it only natural that members of the party would call Hitler their leader, but not in a casual sentence, and in such a reverential tone.

'Why couldn't you leave her in such a position?' Fritz asked. 'Most people allow the authorities to deal with the dead.'

'Most people are not prominent members of Munich society,' Herr Schwarz snapped. 'Most people do not have the press trailing them like dogs.'

'So you took it upon yourself to dispose of Geli's body.'

'I disposed of nothing.' Herr Schwarz sat upright in his chair. His cheeks were flushed. 'I sent her to Vienna, as her mother wished.'

'After contacting the Minister of Justice.'

'We needed papers to get her out of the country.'

'You would have had papers if you had waited for the Kripo.'

'What are you accusing me of, Inspector?'

Fritz studied Herr Schwarz for a moment. His face was such a deep red that he appeared to be overheating. 'I am accusing you of nothing, Herr Schwarz. I am merely curious why you and your friends created more work for me.'

'For you, sir?'

Fritz nodded. 'If you had gone through the normal channels, I would not be here now. You would be at your day's work, and I would be pursuing paperwork on another case. Instead, I sit here, and quite frankly, Herr Schwarz, I do not enjoy it. I find each member of the NSDAP that I deal with to be belligerent and defensive which is beginning to make me think you all have something to hide.'

'We have nothing to hide.'

Fritz smiled. 'See? You are defensive, sir. Tell me, why did Frau Reichert call you?'

'Because she did not know what to do.'

'She said it was because Geli's door was locked and she did not know how to open it.'

'The door was locked,' Herr Schwarz said quickly. 'It was.'

'And you forgot that detail?'

'It seemed unimportant. We told Franz Gürtner of it.'

'You forgot that you kicked in a door?'

'I didn't kick it.'

'Who did?'

'I don't remember.'

'Well, it was either you or Max Amann, wasn't it? Or was someone else there?'

'No one else was there.'

'Then Max kicked in the door. That is, if it was locked in the first place.'

Herr Schwarz took a 'kerchief from his pocket and mopped his brow. 'This feels like an interrogation, Inspector.'

'I'm sorry,' Fritz said. 'It's just that I am trying to resolve this case and I am being thwarted at every turn. Be honest with me, Herr Schwarz. Who smashed Geli's face?'

'Her face?' A drop of sweat ran down his cheek. 'No one.'

'But her nose was broken.'

'The *Münchner Post* lies.'

'I saw her myself, Herr Schwarz.'

Herr Schwarz caught his breath. The room was hot. The goose-neck lamp gave off heat as well as light. Faint sounds of ringing phones travelled up from the floor below. Otherwise the building was silent.

'Didn't Herr Hess tell you? I was certain he would. Since he was at your side when you came to Hitler's apartment on Saturday. He kicked down the door, didn't he? He's the one who took charge of Geli's body. He's the one who accompanied her to Vienna.'

'She hurt her face when she fell,' Herr Schwarz said in a strangled voice.

'How does a woman hurt her face when she falls on her back?'

Another bead of sweat ran down Herr Schwarz's cheek. 'I don't know,' he said. 'I am not a doctor.'

'Clearly,' Fritz said. 'Now, why don't you tell me what really happened?'

Herr Schwarz took a deep breath, then patted at his face daintily with the handkerchief. He cleared his throat. 'Frau Reichert called me to help her. She was afraid for Geli who had not come out of her room since the day before. The door was locked, and she could not get in. I brought Max who apparently called Rudolph. Rudolph kicked in the door, as you said, and there was Geli, dead. We hadn't thought she would be dead. She was willful. We thought she was being difficult because Herr Hitler had left her alone again.'

He took another breath, and closed his eyes. 'She had the gun in her hand. She was clearly dead. We panicked, Inspector. Max mentioned headlines, and we knew that we had to get her out before the newspaper photographers arrived. But by then Frau Winter had arrived, and when she saw Geli, she went for the police. Once the police knew, the reporters would know, so we carried Geli to Max's car and got her away from the apartment.'

'Just like that?'

'No. It was difficult. We had to use the back stairs. For a such a thin girl, she was heavy.'

All the stories were different enough to make Fritz worry. Most witnesses did not alter the chain of events, only the details of those events – what the victim wore, what was in the room. 'So Frau Reichert was afraid for Geli. Why?'

'She did not come to her door after repeated knocks.'

'But you thought Geli was willful.'

'Frau Reichert tends to over dramatise.'

'So she thought something had happened to Geli?'

'She thought Geli had left through her window and run away.'

'From the second floor? It's a twelve-foot drop. Surely the girl wasn't that foolish.'

'No one knew how foolish Geli was.'

'Meaning?'

'It is more logical for the girl to jump than to shoot herself because she cannot go to Vienna.'

'I suppose it is,' Fritz said. He kept his voice even, neutral. 'But perhaps there was another reason for her death?'

'Such as?'

'I did not know her, Herr Schwarz. You did.'

Herr Schwarz opened his eyes and leaned forward. 'There was talk that morning of her being despondent over her first public singing engagement. She was going to go to Vienna to see her coach, but when Herr Hitler demanded that she stay in Munich, she grew even more depressed. She could not face performing without the help. So she died.'

Fritz's clothes felt too tight. The heat in the room was growing. 'It seems such a trivial thing to die over.'

Herr Schwarz shrugged. 'We cannot know what is important to someone else.'

'No, we can't,' Fritz said. 'But it seems odd to me that no one spoke of Geli's upcoming performance or of her fear of it until now. I thought she wanted to go to Vienna to get engaged.'

'The *Münchner Post* again. Inspector, you must not believe all that you read.'

'I don't.' Fritz resisted the urge to loosen his collar. 'I merely get curious when everything I hear contradicts. I didn't even know that Geli was a singer.'

'She wasn't much of one,' Herr Schwarz said. 'It is probably good for Munich that she did not perform.'

'Why is it that everyone I speak to did not like Geli?'

Herr Schwarz stared at Fritz for a long moment. Then he looked down. 'Geli distracted the Führer. If she wanted to shop, he would shop. If she wanted pastries, he found pastries. She was a creature controlled by whim. She had no place in the NSDAP.'

'I didn't realise she was part of the party,' Fritz said.

'She wasn't.' Herr Schwarz clasped his hands on the desktop again. He didn't seem to know what to do with them. 'She was only involved because of her uncle. And even then she was a distraction.'

'It sounds as if you don't mind that she's gone.'

Herr Schwarz sighed. 'I should lie to you, Inspector, and tell you that Geli will be missed, but she won't. Does that mean I opened that door and killed her myself? No. I did not. But to tell you I am sorry about her death is to lie. I am sorry about the way she died, and I think that it is another sign of Geli's selfishness that she killed herself at the exact moment the Führer needed no taint of scandal.'

'Do you think someone could have killed her?'

'I thought you were not interrogating me,' Herr Schwarz said.

'It is a routine question in any case of unusual death,' Fritz said.

The colour in Herr Schwarz's face grew even deeper. 'No,' he said finally. 'I do not think anyone killed her. Who would want to?'

'Gregor Strasser.'

Herr Schwarz laughed, then covered his mouth.

'I do not see what is so funny, Herr Schwarz.'

'Gregor Strasser is a loyal party man. It is his brother Otto who is trouble.'

'Otto?'

'Otto tried to divide the party. But that is old news now.'

Not to Fritz it wasn't. 'He didn't succeed.'

'He went to Berlin with his followers. But he was not very successful. Gregor believes in the Führer. He stayed behind to do what he could. He would not interfere, particularly with Geli.'

'Why not?'

'Because he lacks cunning, Inspector. It takes a devious mind to do such things. He is not devious.'

'But his brother is.'

'His brother is.'

'And where was Otto this weekend?'

Herr Schwarz shrugged. 'I do not keep track of former party members.'

'But you keep track of current members.'

'I try.'

'What of their guns?'

Herr Schwarz froze. 'What of them?'

'Geli was holding a gun when she was found, was she not?'

'I – I believe so.'

'What happened to it?'

A bead of sweat formed on Herr Schwarz's brow. It slowly ran down. He stared at Fritz like an animal startled by sudden light. 'I – ah – I do not know.'

'But you saw it in her hand.'

'Of course.'

'Who removed it?'

'Perhaps no one. Perhaps it was buried with her.'

Fritz shook his head. 'I saw her body, Herr Schwarz. There was no gun.'

'Frau Winter –'

'Has not seen it, and it was not in the apartment. You carried Geli to the car. Was it in her hand then?'

'I – I don't know.'

'But you carried her.'

His gaze skittered away from Fritz's. 'I do not know what happened to the gun.'

'How did you carry her, Herr Schwarz? Wrapped in a blanket? Or was she still alive when you arrived? Did you kill her because she was an embarrassment to the party? Because her relationship with Herr Hitler was not quite proper?'

Herr Schwarz leaned back. 'She was dead.'

'Then how did you carry her?'

'By the feet,' he said. 'I had her feet.'

'But not the gun.'

'Go, please.' Herr Schwarz stood. His shirt stuck to him, the sweat heavy around his armpits. 'This is an illegal interrogation. She killed herself. She is dead. I will say no more.'

Fritz stood too. 'What kind of gun was she holding, Herr Schwarz?'

'You are to leave now,' Herr Schwarz said.

'Surely it can't hurt to tell me that.'

'I do not know guns,' Herr Schwarz said.

'You were in the war, were you not? A soldier knows guns.'

'If you do not leave, I shall call for assistance,' Herr Schwarz said.

Fritz stared at him for a moment. Herr Schwarz was

148

clearly done. He would say no more, and he would contact help if he felt he needed it. Fritz didn't need trouble with the NSDAP – at least no more than he already had.

'I'll go,' Fritz said. 'But you remind your people that a woman died. That is more than an inconvenience. That is a tragedy.'

'Detective –'

Fritz held up his hand, and slowly backed out of the room. 'I thank you for your time,' he said as he stepped into the hall.

It was empty.

He was able to leave the Brown House.

Alone.

TWENTY-ONE

'You thought the political party killed her?' The girl is shocked. She has only studied Demmelmayer, a crime of passion by an intelligent man who thought he could outwit the Kripo. 'To further Hitler?'

'It was not so unusual then.' Fritz is too calm. Atrocity made him calm decades ago. It is a fact which disturbs him only when he thinks of it.

'You thought Strasser killed him.'

'I thought nothing. I was exploring the possibilities.'

'But if the party killed her, it would have been a conspiracy. Against Hitler.'

'Or for him,' Fritz says.

'My God,' she gasps. 'My God.'

'It is not so shocking,' he says dryly, 'when you consider how many people later died for Herr Hitler's ambitions.'

'No.' She speaks slowly, as if she is thinking. 'No, I suppose not. But I thought you were investigating this as a way to discredit Hitler.'

'I had many theories,' he says. 'Perhaps Gregor Strasser killed Geli to discredit Hitler and take over the party. Perhaps one of Hitler's enemies killed her to discredit him. Perhaps the party killed her to get rid of a roadblock to his candidacy. Perhaps her death was accidental.'

'Or someone in the house killed her,' the girl says, caught up now.

Fritz nods, once. 'Or one of Hitler's friends. Or Hitler himself.'

'He would be the logical one,' she says.

'Because of his later history?' Fritz asks.

She nods.

'History does not record him killing anyone with his bare hands.'

'But he was a soldier and he killed millions. He ordered their deaths.'

'He did,' Fritz says. 'You forget one detail.'

'He was out of the city when she died.'

'Exactly.' Fritz smiles. The expression feels tight on his face. She stares at him, as if waiting for him to go on, as if he will tell her the result before he reaches the end of his story.

'You were going to get Photostats of the articles.' He does not mind letting her take those. He can get other copies. It is the letters he minds. The letters and the photographs.

His remark makes her glance at her watch. 'I'd have to leave now.'

'Go,' he says. Then more gently, 'Go. I will still be here tomorrow.'

She nods and packs her things. He watches her small movements, domestic and tidy. Now he wishes that he had watched her cook. Such a rare thing to have a woman take care of him. He cannot remember the last time — before the war, perhaps. His mother used to make soup when he was ill as a boy. His mother. She too died in the starvation after the war.

The girl turns, seems about to say something but he shakes his head just enough to keep her silent. 'Tomorrow I will provide the pastries,' he says.

She laughs and then lets herself out, taking the energy from the room with her. He sits in the fading sunlight, feeling alone for the first time since those awful days after Gisela left. Then the solitude was a physical thing, something to be fought with activity and rigorous exercise. And he has not been out of the apartment in days. Rigorous exercise – at least his old man's version – is a good idea.

He gets up, takes his dishes to the sink, and grabs his coat off the coat rack. He double-checks the pocket for his keys, finds them, and lets himself out.

The hallway is dark and smells of cabbage. The building has aged since he moved in, years before. Then it had seemed smart to rent while owning land outside of Munich. Now he wonders if he shouldn't have built that house, as he had once planned. He would not have the city for company, but he would not have loud loutish neighbours either. He takes the stairs two at a time, gripping the wobbly wood banister as he goes down. When he reaches the street, he stops, takes a breath, and blinks in the brightness.

Munich has changed over the decades. Skyscrapers tower over buildings that have existed for hundreds of years. When the monks from Tegernsee settled on the Isar they never imagined that the site of their diocese would become a bustling place of wood, steel and glass. The sound of construction fills the city from morning to night. Munich will hold the Olympics, and the event will purify the city, wipe away the past.

If only it were so easy.

He glances down the concrete sidewalk to his favourite beer hall. It has changed ownership a dozen times since he first went inside in 1925, but it has not changed much. The food is the same: Weisswürscht, Brez'n, and sweet mustard served with good

Bavarian beer. The inside has steel counters in the kitchen, but out front the wood is worn and the walls still covered with paintings from the reign of Ludwig the Second. Fritz stares at the sign, repainted a decade ago in nineteenth-century style but somehow having lost its charm, and he realises that he does not want to sit alone in a place of merriment. The disquiet that has haunted him since he saw Wilhelm's picture the day before colours each waking moment. Fritz does not know when he stopped living. He became famous long after Wilhelm died, but his only hope for joy starved to death in 1919. If he closes his eyes, he can still see Wilhelm's face, skin drawn tight against the skull, eyes too big, too pale and tired to even ask for help.

Fritz sighs. Open the door to the past and all the memories crowd to the entrance. He should have stuck with Demmelmayer. He can recite the facts of the case in his sleep, explain his role in the simplest of terms. But he had to start telling the girl about Geli Raubal, digging through his boxes, and seeing his photographs again for the first time in years. It is bad enough that memories live on the streets of Munich, but now they also live in his own mind.

Before he knows it, he is walking away from the beer hall. His unplanned steps, guided more by memory than by any rational purpose, take him around the English Garden. He stops in a neighbourhood he has not walked through in decades. Prinzregentenplaz.

The building still stands. In fact, the street does not look much different. The cars are newer, smaller, and faster. Next door is a modern complex of glass and steel, looking to him like an American about to destroy a tradition. Boys with green and orange hair ride past on bicycles. The building has a layer of sooty grey it did not *have in its glory years, the result of too many car exhausts, too much smog. Official signs mark the doorway. He crosses the street and stands before it.*

So many changes. The street has the same general feel, but it is not the same. Buildings once home to Munich's elite now house clinics, solicitors, and advertising agencies. This building, though, whose residents he once envied for their comfort, this building which had seemed to him in his early days in Kripo, long before he became famous, a symbol of wealth he wanted to achieve is now owned by the government. Friends of his have worked inside. On the second floor, the sign says, is the traffic fines office for the city of Munich.

He does not go inside. He cannot. He wonders about the man who works in Geli's old room. Does he know that below the carpet, the furniture, on the formerly polished wood floor, lies the permanent stain of blood from a woman who died violently? Does her ghost appear to him? Does she wander through the offices, searching for her canary, Hansi, or does she yell in defiance when her uncle tries to imprison her again?

Munich is an old city, full of ghosts. His apartment building dates from those dark days before the war. So much had happened before he moved in. He never looked under the threadbare grey carpet, never searched for blood spatters appearing through the paint coats on the walls. Someone could have died in his place and he would never know.

The thought only adds to his melancholy. Men come out the door wearing overcoats despite the day's warmth. Women emerge, looking preoccupied, carrying bags under their arms. They walk beside him as if it is common for an old man to stand on the sidewalk staring at a government building. Perhaps it is. No one wants to pay his fines, not even old men, especially not old men who should know better.

He is like a ghost to them, already barely visible, and certainly unimportant to the hustle and bustle of their daily lives. No. Ghosts only become visible to the aging when they have a chance to reflect on their lives, their failures, and the chances they have missed.

TWENTY-TWO

He met Henrich in the English Garden, near the Chinese Tower. Because Fritz had not eaten much that day, he bought himself some sausage, sauerkraut, and a stein of beer to wash it down. He sat at one of the wooden tables in the shadow of the pagoda roof, and watched the crowd. Once he had enjoyed coming here. Now he came when he had business to do. It was a good place to meet other officers and to discuss things he did not want discussed in the precinct.

The sun was warm, and since it was mid-morning, the crowd was slight. A Communist stood on a box in the meadow, speaking to a handful of people, his voice carried away by the wind. Women tugged tiny caps on their babies. Men walked by in pairs, discussing the day. An old man leaned off the second floor railing in the tower and watched the crowd pass. Fritz saw no member of the NSDAP.

Henrich arrived a few minutes later. He was wearing an overcoat, brown pants and regular shoes, his head covered with a beret. He licked his fingers and tossed away a food wrapper as he approached. He too had taken advantage of the Garden in order to eat his lunch.

When he saw Fritz, he smiled.

'That woman,' Henrich said as he approached, 'is one of the most difficult I have ever met.'

'Wouldn't she give you the letter?'

'She wouldn't even let me into the apartment. When she found out I came from you, she told me to give you a message: if you are to work with her, *you* are to work with her.'

Fritz sighed. He had wanted that letter.

'But,' Henrich said with a smile, 'I got the letter from her. I let her know I could make her life quite difficult. I could bring an entire team of political police down on them if I even implied the death of the girl had anything to do with politics.'

In spite of himself, Fritz smiled. He hadn't wanted to be so hard-handed with the witnesses, but he was finding he had no choice. They were not cooperating.

'Did she tell you anything else?' he asked, holding his hand out for the letter.

'Only if I come again, I can go to hell.' Henrich shrugged. 'One little *hausfrau* does not frighten me.' He reached into the pocket of his overcoat and removed a tattered piece of paper. It had been taped together quickly, leaving little tape patches where paper should have been. But it was still readable.

Fritz took it from Henrich and studied it. It read:

Dear Herr Hitler,

Thank you again for the wonderful invitation to the theatre. It was a memorable evening. I am most grateful to you for your kindness. I am counting the hours until I may have the joy of another meeting.

Yours,

Eva

'Did you think to get a sample of Frau Winter's hand-writing?' Fritz asked.

'We have her information at the precinct from when we brought her in. I had time, so I went and compared. If that old woman wrote this, she is very talented.'

Fritz stroked the page. The tape nearly covered it all. Someone had shredded it, and someone else had taken a lot of work to piece it all together again. 'Do we have any idea who Eva is?'

Henrich rolled his eyes. 'That took some wheedling. Frau Winter sees information as coin.'

'You had to pay her?'

Henrich shook his head. 'We came to an understanding, the old woman and I. I would not ask her questions about Adolf Hitler or try to enter the apartment, and she would not withhold information from me. This was a tacit thing which evolved over the course of the morning.'

Fritz let out a mouthful of air. He was lucky he had sent Henrich to see Frau Winter. Another detective, less versed in subtlety, would have ruined this lead altogether. 'So tell me who this Eva is.'

'She is a shopgirl that Hitler has been seeing on the side for two years. It is an on-again off-again thing, which Geli was quite jealous of, according to Frau Winter. When Hitler took out Eva, he did not have time for Geli.'

'You know no more than that?'

'Oh, no.' Henrich smiled. He waved another small piece of paper at Fritz. 'I have her address.'

He has forgotten breakfast until five minutes before the girl is scheduled to arrive. She has never been late before, and she will be surprised to discover him away. He tacks a note to the door, and hurries down the stairs to the good bakery at the corner.

The inside smells of küchen and freshly made bread. His mouth waters. In his wanderings the night before, he only managed to eat a bit of schweinswürstl at the Chinese Tower. There he thought of Henrich. Dear Henrich, who never completely understood those last few months of 1931, although he remained faithful until the end.

Fritz orders some strudel and küchen, and watches as the woman behind the counter places the pastries in a white bag. He gets two coffees as well, and carries the entire package back to his apartment.

The girl is inside, setting up her tape recorder. She smiles at him. 'The articles are in the Münchner Post.'

Of course they are, he wants to say to her. Do you think I was lying? Trying to make myself a big man? But he says nothing. He hands her a coffee, sets his near his chair, and puts the bag on the table between them.

'But after September 25, they stop.' She takes a piece of küchen and sits across from him. 'I couldn't find anything else. Not even in the histories. Hitler's biographies mention this only in passing. One went so far as to say that Geli's death made Hitler suicidal.'

Fritz takes some strudel. Frosting will always be his downfall. Thick or glazed, white or dark, he loves liquid sugar on top of the sweets. 'The answers you look for are not in the papers or in the histories. Historians do not know the truth.'

'I assume they did research. I assume they did all the appropriate primary research.' She takes a bite, and wipes a crumb from her lip.

'They did not,' he says.

'How do you know?'

He looks at her for a moment, then says, 'None of them has spoken to me.'

'Perhaps the case isn't as important as you think.'

'You have not heard it all,' he says.

'If it were important —'

'Remember what I told you,' he says. 'No one speaks of important things.'

She pulls another piece off her pastry, her brow furrowed. She hunches in her chair, thinking, worrying that this case is not worth all the time they have spent. He can see that in her eyes. She wants another Demmelmayer.

Gustav Demmelmayer killed his wife and covered the murder very well. Fritz solved it using techniques not available before the war: comparing hairs from the killer to hairs found under his wife's fingernails, taking fingerprints from the brass buttons on her coat, and matching the contents of her stomach to the meal in the trash behind Demmelmayer's home. It was, in its own way, a simple case, no different from any other domestic murder in Munich that year. The husband suspects the wife of adultery, confronts her, kills her, and dumps the body. Hundreds of husbands did the same after the war, some with more cause. Some whose wives left, and sold themselves for bits of bread.

Demmelmayer was different only in that he cleaned up the murder site instead of fleeing from it. He threw the body in the Isar, and managed to commit his crime unwitnessed. He made two mistakes: he destroyed and then replaced the kitchen knife he had used to kill her — and the woman who sold him the replacement remembered the date; and he placed his wife's body in a leather garment bag weighted with stones but did not toss her deep enough in the river. The body was discovered, mostly dry, soon after it had been disposed of.

Some men's wives were never found. Some of those women became anonymous bodies at city morgues. Many of the detectives in the Kripos across Germany did not understand this scenario.

But Fritz did, and thus his fame, and the case known as Demmelmayer was born.

The Raubal case, on the other hand, had none of the common elements. It was a challenge, a special case, the kind most detectives never see, the kind with implications far beyond a family squabble. Hitler headed a political party. He had an alibi and many enemies. This case, not Demmelmayer, should have been the case Fritz was famous for.

'Not important,' he says as he takes another strudel. 'No, child, it was so important the papers were afraid of it, afraid of what they might discover. Don't you understand what we were dealing with here?'

'Adolf Hitler before he came to power.'

Fritz shakes his head. 'Adolf Hitler as he came to power.'

'What's the distinction?'

He pauses, pulls another piece of küchen apart with his unfamiliar fingers. 'You will soon understand the distinction. If you listen.'

'I just wish you wouldn't be so mysterious.'

'And I wish you wouldn't be so impatient.' He leans back in his chair and closes his eyes, biting back the rage that flares like a live thing inside him. He was a fool for choosing an ignorant American. A woman who might have been his granddaughter.

He should have chosen a German who had family to go to,

162

someone who could explain the horrible years after the war, the lack of food, the years that money became worthless, the influx of rich foreigners. The schiebers and their tricks getting wealthy off the pain of others. He should have chosen someone who understood that sometimes words were the only thing a man could believe in, when his future and his past lay in tatters at his feet. Someone who would understand the silences, the nuances, as much as he understood the culture itself.

But he has not. He has chosen her, and she at least is interested. She simply wants to know his focus, where this story is going. She knows the end of Demmelmayer. She believes the ending of this case will be as simple.

He opens his eyes and leans forward. She is watching him, the last bit of küchen between her thumb and forefinger.

'This is not Demmelmayer,' he says. 'This is something more and something less. This is a case you cannot understand without understanding the details, without hearing the facts in the order that I learned them. I thought you wanted to know about the detective's mind.'

She eats the küchen. 'I do,' she says softly.

'Then listen,' he says. 'And understand. The papers were silenced. Some with threats of lawsuit. Some with threats. And what could they do? The body was buried. The death was ruled a suicide. My investigation was unofficial, and I was only speaking to people involved in NSDAP. They would not run to the papers with news of my inquiry. Historians cannot know of this. I have the records.'

'And no one has spoken to you?'

'What would lead them to me? And why would they have

interest? They do not know the importance of this case any more than you do.'

She bows her head at the rebuke. Then she sighs, nods once, and presses the 'record' button on her tape machine.

'So,' she says, a bit too brightly, as if she is trying to make the tense moment pass, 'who gave you the paintings?'

Fritz sighs and shakes his head. She is over-eager and under-educated. 'In due time,' he says. 'We first had to solve the mystery of the letter.'

He tells her of Henrich and the mysterious Eva.

'Eva Braun?' the girl asks.

'Eva Braun,' he says, 'long before she became famous.'

TWENTY-THREE

Henrich took him to a photographic shop. The storefront was recessed against the neighbouring shops, and even from the doorway it looked dark and uninviting. The photographs in the two slim windows which flanked the door were varied. Some were tasteful art shots of Bavarian women: not too pretty but made striking by use of lighting and make-up. Others were of soldiers looking tall and proud in their uniforms, and families huddled stiffly and sombrely together. Only a photograph of Hitler – showing a thinner, younger man than the one Fritz had met, looking fierce and holding the passenger door of an automobile – gave any indication that Hoffman Photographic Studio did anything other than studio portraits.

Fritz went inside. To his right was a small sitting room. Lamps with umbrella-like shades and cameras on stands broke the illusion. In front of Fritz was a single desk with a middle-aged woman sitting behind it. She did not smile at him when he entered. Behind her were rows and rows of portraits, all expensively framed, all difficult to see in the dim light.

Henrich hesitated beside him. Fritz stuck his hands in the pockets of his overcoat and approached the woman. 'I am looking for Eva Braun. I am told she works here.'

The woman said nothing. She stood and slipped through a curtain into the back room. Her movements filled the air with strong perfume and the sharp scent of emulsifier. Henrich glanced at Fritz and shrugged. After a moment, a short blonde with athletic grace entered the room. She wore a black A-line skirt and heels that accentuated her muscular legs. The black and white striped sweater made her appear slimmer than she was. She wore her hair in a modified marcel that revealed her youth. Fritz guessed her age to be 19.

'I am Eva,' she said.

Fritz nodded to her. 'Fraulein, I am Detective Inspector Stecher. Is there a place we may talk privately?'

Eva's eyes widened. She glanced at the woman who did not look at her.

'In the back,' Eva finally said.

The older woman took her seat behind the desk, as if she expected a flood of customers. Eva parted a curtain and waited for the two men. Fritz slipped around the desk and stepped into the back. It was half the size of the front with a door labelled 'Darkroom' on the left and a smaller room to the right. He waited for the girl. She led Fritz and Henrich into the smaller room. The walls were covered with cabinets, and they had to squeeze to get around the table in the centre.

Eva offered them some bread still sitting on a sideboard, but Fritz and Henrich declined.

'Is it private back here?' Henrich asked.

The girl bit her lower lip. She was obviously worried about herself. 'Frau Hoffmann can't hear.'

Fritz wasn't certain if that statement meant that the older woman couldn't hear at all or if she couldn't hear what was being discussed in the back room. He supposed it didn't matter.

'We would like to talk with you about the death of Geli Raubal,' he said.

'Oh.' Eva sat down. She crossed her ankles and tucked her legs under her chair, an unconscious way of emphasising her strongest feature.

'Did you know her?' Henrich asked.

'No.' The edges of the girl's mouth tightened, as if she had to restrain herself from saying more.

Fritz sat down across from her. The chair was old and wobbly. He braced himself to keep from swaying. Henrich sat as well.

'Did you know of her?' Fritz asked.

Eva nodded. 'She is Adolf Hitler's niece.'

Is. Eva was one of the few people to speak of Geli in the present tense. 'I understand that you know Herr Hitler,' Fritz said.

'He comes to the shop.'

'He has taken you out a few times, no?' Henrich said.

She glanced at him like a doe trapped in a hunter's sights. 'Who said that?'

'You did.' Fritz removed the taped letter from his pocket. Eva watched his movements closely. He slid the letter across the table. 'Did you write that?'

She put a small hand on the letter, her finger tracing the tape. 'What happened to it?'

'I was hoping you knew.'

Her finger followed the jagged lines formed by the rips. It lingered over Hitler's name. 'I sent it to Herr Hitler. I haven't seen it since.'

'Did he respond to it?'

A small smile played at the edges of her mouth before she suppressed it. 'He had Herr Hoffman bring me flowers.'

The statement surprised Fritz, although he did not allow his surprise to show. Hitler had not struck him as a sentimental man. 'How long have you known Herr Hitler?'

'Two years.' Her finger kept moving, up, down, over, around. Her wrist bone was visible and she had muscle definition in her forearm. She was athletic in a way that Geli had not been.

'And you dated Herr Hitler all this time?'

This time she allowed her smile. Before she answered, she gazed up at Fritz from the corner of her eyes. A sly, flirtatious look. 'I didn't know who he was at first.'

Henrich shot a disbelieving glance at Fritz. No one who paid attention to life in Munich would have failed to recognise Hitler, even two years ago. Eva's revelation only confirmed Fritz's sense of her youth. 'How did you meet?'

'He came to the shop with Herr Hoffman. They sat opposite me. Herr Hitler was watching my legs. I felt slightly embarrassed because I had shortened my skirt that day, and I wasn't sure I'd got the hem right.' As she spoke, she tugged at the hem of the skirt she was wearing, adjusting it over her calves. 'We talked for a while, and I refused his offer of a lift in his Mercedes. That was when Herr Hoffman told me who he was. He came back to the shop a lot after that. He brought me candy.'

'You never met his niece?'

A slight flush built in her cheeks. It added to the freshness of her looks, made her look windblown and alive. 'I never went to his apartment. When he took me out, we had our own places.'

'Did you meet any of his friends?'

'I work for Herr Hoffman. He is with Herr Hitler all the time.'

'But you never met any of his other friends.'

Her hand brushed her skirt. She looked back down at the letter. 'I am not political,' she said. 'I am for him to relax.'

Fritz stiffened. She was parroting the words. All of Hitler's associates seemed to quote him without attribution. He would like some time alone with the man, just to get a sense about how they managed to do that.

'So you were his mistress?' Henrich said. Fritz drew in his breath sharply. He did not want to antagonise this girl.

'No!' Eva's flush grew deeper. 'He was going to marry me!'

Fritz frowned. No one else had mentioned that. 'He proposed to you?'

Her lips tightened into a small bow. She pushed the letter away.

'Fraulein, this is important,' Henrich said. 'Did he propose to you?'

'He was going to marry me.' Her tone had a petulant edge, as if she expected their disbelief. The tense bothered

169

Fritz again. She spoke of Geli in the present tense, but Hitler in the past.

'When was the last time you saw him?' Fritz asked.

'A few weeks ago.'

'Then you sent him the letter?' Henrich said. 'It seems formal for a girl to send to her fiancé.'

'He isn't my fiancé,' she said. 'He *was*.'

Her cheeks were ruddy, almost scarlet, and the flush had crept to her throat. Clearly, the man had lied to her to get her to sleep with him. Fritz suppressed a sigh. Such things were not unusual, and he disliked her distress. The girl's relationship with Hitler didn't matter unless she had access to the apartment and to one of Hitler's guns. 'Do you have a key to his apartment?'

She shook her head. With three fingers, she pulled the letter toward her, touching it as if it were a talisman. 'I don't even know where he lives. On Prinzregentenstrasse, I think. But if I delivered photographs or if I met him, it was here or at the Brown House.'

'You have never been to his apartment?'

'No!' She looked up, her eyes wet, her humiliation palpable. 'I am not that kind of girl.'

Fritz swallowed, knowing his next questions would increase her upset, but unable to see any way around them. 'Did you know of his relationship with Geli Raubal?'

'She is his niece. Everyone knows that.'

'I was told,' Fritz said slowly, 'that he was in love with her.'

'No!' Eva's lower lip was trembling. Her eyes narrowed and filled with tears. 'He loves me!'

170

'His housekeeper says that Geli tore up your note out of jealousy.' Henrich leaned forward as he spoke almost as if he were going to comfort the girl.

'No.' The word was a whisper.

'He never took you to any public meeting, to meet his friends, to see his apartment?' Fritz asked.

A tear ran down her left cheek. 'He loves me,' she said again. 'I am for him to relax. I help him. He loves me.'

'Did you ever see him with Geli Raubal?'

She shook her head. Another tear escaped, this time from her right eye. 'He can't love his niece like he would love me. He can't. She's his niece.' Then she swallowed. 'Who told you these lies?'

'Most of the people who knew him also knew he was in love with Geli.'

'And that's why he wouldn't take me out like a proper woman?' Her voice was small, childish, needy. In that single sentence, Fritz understood that she had never known about her competition.

'His housekeeper says Geli was jealous of you.'

'Good,' Eva said. Her chin jutted out. 'Good.'

'So jealous she tore up your letter,' Henrich added.

Eva put her hand over the letter in a protective gesture. 'She found it?'

'The housekeeper says that's why Geli killed herself, because she was jealous of you.'

Eva wiped the tears off her cheek. Her colour was fading. 'She was? Of me?' The needy voice, the little girl voice again. Eva had to believe this.

171

Fritz nodded.

'So why come to see me?' Eva said. 'It seems obvious.'

'Because,' Fritz said softly, 'someone broke Geli's nose before she died.'

'Oh, he would never do that,' Eva said.

Her response made Fritz lean forward, his heart beating faster. He had expected surprise from her, the thought that Geli had been murdered, not this quick and almost automatic denial. 'Who would never do that?'

'Herr Hitler. He would never.' She glanced from Fritz to Henrich and then back to Fritz. 'That is what you were going to ask me, isn't it?'

'What made you think we were going to ask about Herr Hitler?' Fritz asked.

'That's why you're here, isn't it? About Herr Hitler? I don't know his niece.'

'Do you think he could have hurt her?'

She slid her chair back, just enough to be noticeable. The flush had receded from her face, and her skin had turned an odd, pasty white. She looked terrified. 'I didn't say that.'

'I am asking you,' Fritz said.

'No, of course not,' she said. 'He never hurts anyone.'

'Then who do you think killed Geli?'

Eva opened her mouth, then closed it. She glanced at Henrich who did not move. 'I thought you said she killed herself. Because of me.'

Fritz let out the breath he had been holding. The girl lacked guile. 'So I did,' he said.

The girl bit her lower lip and nodded. Fritz stood, and

Henrich did the same. He held out his hand. It took a moment before she slid the letter back to him. Then she stood too.

'Thank you,' he said, as he put the letter back into his pocket. 'I appreciate your help.'

She did not move. He nodded to Henrich, who went through the door. Fritz stopped when he reached the tiny hallway, turned and looked at Eva. She was sitting at the table, staring at her hands.

'Eva,' he said.

She looked up, her lashes wet, her eyes red-rimmed.

'The next time he hurts you, send for me. I will help.'

The flush returned, deep and swift. 'He doesn't hurt me,' she whispered. 'He's never hurt me at all.'

TWENTY-FOUR

'*B*ut you think he did,' the girl says, breaking into his narrative. '*I have seen such things before. She would not have denied so quickly if he had been a gentle man.*' Fritz uses the moment to get up and walk to the kitchen. His throat is always dry now. He decides not to wait for a decent hour. He wants a beer, and so he pours himself one in a jelly glass.

'*Eva wrote the note, then?*'

The sip is warm, soothing. He closes his eyes as the alcohol burns its way down his throat. '*She did.*'

'*Doesn't that prove that she was his mistress then, not Geli?*'

'*It proved nothing. As we left, the woman in front was waiting for us. She was Hoffman's wife, and she did not like Eva much, in that way women have.*'

'*What way?*' The girl's tone has an edge. He is beginning to understand that she hates it when he generalises about women.

'*She was friendly enough, let her work there, maybe even confided in her. But underneath, she didn't trust her, didn't even like her much.*'

'*You got all that from one conversation?*'

He shrugs. He has no answer for that. He was good at what he

175

did. He can understand what people feel if he concentrates on it. That is part of his gift he never talks about. It is the part no one will believe, just as the girl, this Annie, does not believe it. 'She had no reason to tell us otherwise.'

'Tell you what?'

'That Eva was lying.'

'About Hitler?'

'About her relationship with him.' Fritz takes another sip, then pours more into the glass before returning to his chair. He sets the glass beside the full ashtray. He is getting hungry. Soon they should have lunch. This time he will not let her cook for him. 'Hitler "escorted" Eva, but never proposed. In fact, when Eva began bragging around the shop that she was Hitler's mistress and he was going to marry her, Herr Hoffman told her to stop telling lies or he would fire her.'

'Was she lying?'

'She stopped saying anything, and for a year Hitler insisted that all his photographs be delivered to him. He did not want to see Eva. Then in the summer before Geli's death, he showed up again and spent some time with Eva. Not enough, though, for her. Hence the note.'

The girl pushes the pause button on her recorder. 'May I have some of that beer?'

'My house is yours,' he says.

She gets up, and takes a stein from his cupboard. She picks his favourite, the one he lets no one else touch. But he says nothing. He does not want to add to the tension he feels from her today.

'So Hitler hit Geli,' she says. 'But he could not have killed her.'

'Why do you say that?' he asks.

'Because you were on the case. You solved it.' Her naiveté surprises him. 'And he could not have gone on if he had done such a thing.'

She brings the stein back to her chair, then releases the pause button so the recorder starts again.

'You are certain of that?' Fritz asks. 'None of your leaders have committed crimes?'

'No, of course not,' she says, with a primness that makes him smile. 'Are you so certain?'

'You're saying he did it, and no one brought him to justice?'

'I am saying nothing. At this point in the case, I knew nothing for certain.'

'Why didn't you go to Hitler directly? He would have been the one to tell you about all his women and what he was doing when Geli died.'

Fritz nods. 'He would have, but by then he had disappeared.'

TWENTY-FIVE

'We are receiving complaints about the way you're spending your vacation.' The Chief Inspector's wire-rimmed glasses had slipped to the edge of his nose. He leaned back in his chair. His sleeves were pushed up to his elbows, and the cuffs were smudged with ink.

'I thought you were going to handle those complaints.'

'And I have been. What a man does on his own time is his own business.' The Chief pushed up his glasses with the knuckle of his right forefinger. 'But I had thought you would be a bit more discreet.'

'This case is making discretion impossible.' Fritz sighed and sat down. The Chief's office was hot. Someone had turned on the heat in the building even though the afternoon was warm. 'And now I think I'm going to need the help of the political branch.'

The Chief placed his hands on his thighs – a deliberate gesture designed to prevent an involuntary response. Fritz had seen him use it before, each time in a trying situation.

'Why?' the Chief asked.

'Because I cannot find Hitler and I don't know where to look.' Fritz pulled his chair closer to the desk. The metal legs dragged on the wooden floor, scratching it. The Chief looked pained even though he couldn't see the damage.

'I thought, from all the complaints I've been getting, that you spoke to him already.'

'Briefly,' Fritz said. 'On Saturday. He said he would see me on Sunday, but I was already in Vienna. It wouldn't have mattered. I heard from Schupo that he left the apartment before dawn on Sunday morning and hasn't been back.'

'Then who wrote the letter in the *Münchner Post*?' the Chief asked.

Fritz shrugged. 'It could have been Hitler. It could have been his men. I don't know. I do know that I need to talk with him, and he has disappeared from Munich. None of my sources know where he is, but I rarely work on political cases. I need the help of the Political Branch.'

The Chief took off his glasses and sucked on the earguard. His face looked naked without them, younger, as if he were revealing a part of himself no one else saw. 'Have you evidence that links him with Angela Raubal's death?'

Fritz shook his head. 'I have information that links everyone from a 19-year-old jealous shopgirl to political enemies of Hitler to intimations of Hitler himself. If I could talk with the man, I might get a sense of what happened.'

'What sense have you now?'

Fritz leaned against the desk. The wood had absorbed the warmth of the room. The papers nearest him smelled of pipe tobacco, even though the Chief didn't smoke.

'Hitler's people are covering up the crime,' Fritz said. 'But I do not know if they are doing so merely to avoid a scandal

180

planned by opposing parties, or if they are doing so to protect one of their own.'

'The shopgirl?'

Fritz shook his head. 'A lover of Hitler's, perhaps, but she was startled enough by the news of his affection for his niece that I can rule her out. Also, the housekeeper used the girl as a reason for the niece's suicide. I think they are trying to lead me down a blind alley.'

'I don't want you to talk with Hitler until you have something concrete,' the Chief said. 'It is difficult enough to interview a political candidate, particularly one with the kind of connections that Hitler has. The last thing we want is for this unofficial investigation to be forced to a conclusion.'

Fritz sighed. This investigation had given him a sense of unease from the moment he walked into the apartment on Prinzregentenplaz. 'You tell me I need to work this case, and then you tie my hands. What do you want here, Chief? Are you hoping that I will find Hitler to be the murderer?'

The Chief stared at something over Fritz's head for so long that at first it seemed as if he hadn't heard. Then the Chief said, 'A year ago, in Berlin, members of the NSDAP kicked my younger sister to death. They claimed she had threatened them, but witnesses said the men were baiting her, calling her names like jewbait, schieber, and kike –'

*

'Schieber?' the girl says. 'You have used the word "schieber".'

'Ach.' Fritz takes a sip of beer. He does not want to be sidetracked now. He wants her to listen. Is that too much to ask. 'Not all schiebers were Jews.'

181

'Then why was the Chief offended by this?'

The exasperation makes him stand. He paces around the small apartment, his fists clenched. 'Because the schiebers got rich after the war. They took food from the mouths of children and sold it for profit. After the war, any German who was well fed was probably a schieber. It was a shameful thing.'

'And the NSDAP called her a schieber because she was Jewish, because Jews stereotypically get rich off other people's pain, because –'

'I did not make up the rule or the story. And I did not mention the stereotype. You did.' Fritz stops behind her chair. His fists are clenched so hard his nails have dug into his palm. 'Just because I am a German of a certain age, I am judged anti-Semitic. Let me remind you. I spent the years you have read about, the years of the atrocities before the war, and the years of the war, in London.'

'It does not automatically provide a defence,' she says. 'The attitude was prevalent. Even I know that –'

'I have enough guilt without adding this,' he says. A drop of blood falls from his right palm onto the back of the chair. 'I warned you that this story is not pretty. It is not pretty for women, or Jews, or Germans, for that matter. If you do not want to hear any more, I would be glad to take your tapes and apologise for the use of your time. I will talk about Demmelmayer and we never have to see each other again.'

When he finishes, the room is so quiet all he can hear is his own breathing. Somewhere in the middle of his rant, she has paused the recorder.

'Why have you chosen to tell this to me?'

He stands behind her. She is wearing a light perfume, flowery, very feminine. He can lie to her. He can say he is reminiscing *because he is getting old, because the story needs to be told, because she is the only one who appeared even slightly interested. But he has got into the habit of telling her everything. So he says, 'I tell you because you remind me of her.'*

'Of Geli?'

'No,' he says, and returns to his chair.

*

'– then,' the Chief said, 'when she ignored them and kept trying to walk down the street, they grabbed her, beat her and kicked her to death.'

'I'm sorry,' Fritz said, hoping he sounded sincere.

It had become a litany through the Twenties. Somewhere around 1925, people stopped talking about their personal grief because the collective grief was too overwhelming. Compassion had become a rare commodity. Fritz still had trouble feeling it, although he knew that the Chief wanted something from him.

The Chief did not appear to have heard him. 'The witnesses were bribed, the case closed from lack of evidence. I am not naïve. Perhaps I would have understood the difficulties the Berlin force had. Lord knows how many cases we have had here where the witnesses have been silenced, the criminals have disappeared. But Hitler –' the Chief took a deep breath '– Hitler said that decent women cannot walk the street when there are Jews around, that it is up to all Germans to banish the Jewish scourge from the face of Germany, that my sister's death was merely part – *part* – of what all Jews deserved. No sorrow. No remorse. Just a pledge to continue the slaughter and the persecution.'

'So this is a personal vendetta,' Fritz said.

The Chief blinked and looked at him as if remembering he were there. 'No,' the Chief said. 'Yes. Perhaps. All I know is that the NSDAP is a cancer among us and if we allow them to grow, then my sister's death will become one of many.'

She already was one of many, but Fritz did not say that. Instead, he moved away from the desk. 'I cannot conduct a secret investigation so that you can get revenge.'

'I don't want that kind of revenge,' the Chief said. 'I don't care if Hitler pays for this. I just want to prevent the NSDAP from covering up another murder, especially one that might destroy their power.'

'Sir, it would seem to me that those are not the right reasons to conduct an investigation.'

The Chief slipped his glasses back on, taking the vulnerable edge from his face. He leaned forward. 'You took those pictures of Angela Raubal. Someone beat her before she died. You concluded that she was murdered. When someone is murdered in Munich, the case is handled by the Kripo, no?'

'Yes, but sometimes those cases are closed, like this one was, and ruled something other –'

'Only the Kripo had no say in the Minister of Justice's ruling, did they?'

'No, sir.'

'We never even had a chance to investigate, did we?'

'No, sir.'

'A girl was murdered in the home of a political candidate with enough clout to cover over that murder. In the last election, his party gained 95 seats in the Reichstag. In the next election, they could gain more. Germany is already considered a nation of thugs. We are bent under reparations and –'

'Sir, this could cost me my career.'

The Chief stopped. He crossed his arms, and looked down his long nose at Fritz. 'Yes, it could,' he said. 'You work for me, not for Franz Gürtner or Adolf Hitler.'

'But if anyone gets in trouble for this investigation, it will be me.'

The Chief shook his head. 'All of Munich knows that no one in Kripo takes a piss without my permission. You inflate your position here. The complaints have been coming to me, and will continue to do so. I would simply like there to be fewer of them.'

Fritz's hands were shaking. Instead of reassuring him, the conversation made him feel even more alone. He stood. 'Will I be able to get assistance from the Political Branch?'

The Chief stared at him for a moment. 'I will have them find Herr Hitler for you. But you will not learn of his location until you have a suspect and clear evidence.'

'Sir, I need to talk with Hitler.'

'You need to continue your investigation. Quietly.' And with that, Fritz was dismissed.

TWENTY-SIX

'*H*e *put you in an impossible position,*' *the girl says.* '*Why didn't you resign?*'

'*Why are you asking so many questions today?*' *Fritz's glass is empty. The beer has left a sour taste in his mouth.*

'*Because I don't understand. If I knew more about the case, perhaps I would be able to make some of the logical jumps —*'

'*No.*' *He shakes his head.* '*It is more than that. You are angry with me. Do you think I waste your time?*'

She is looking down at her hands.

'*Do you think this is unimportant?*'

'*I think,*' *she says softly,* '*you are using this case to prove that you are more important than I think you are.*'

He lets out a breath and leans back. '*But you said this was insignificant before.*'

'*I merely want you to tell me the point.*'

'*I do not know what the point is.*' *As soon as the sentence leaves him, he realises his mistake.*

She shuts off the recorder. But he does not want her to leave.

'*Please,*' *he says.* '*Please, understand. You are the scholar. Scholars analyse. Scholars determine what is important and what is not. But sometimes scholars do not know everything. Please. This case is crucial to Bavaria. To Germany. You must know what happened.'*

'Did they force you to leave? Did you discover who the murderer was and did the Minister of Justice ask you to leave the force?'

'It was not so simple. I retired. I knew I could do no more.'

'Yet you would not resign when the Chief Inspector made you the tool of his vengeance.'

Fritz gripped the arms of his chair. 'If you are such an expert on the Bavarian police, you would know why I did not resign then.'

'Why?'

'Because I was afraid I would starve.'

The words hang between them. She has gathered her bag closer, like she does when she is about to leave. 'But you said you saved money in that period.'

'And the inflation was starting again. Five million unemployed at the start of 1931, and a million more by 1932. It seemed like 1925 all over again. And 1919. I will be someone's slave before I go hungry again.'

'But you retired six months later –' She stops herself. 'My God,' she says and lets her bag drop. 'Did something happen so that you could afford to retire six months later?'

He does not answer that. He has no simple answer. Everything is infinitely more complex than she makes it. Perhaps her mind lacks the ability to grasp the subtleties of life.

'Let me get us lunch,' he says, and flees out the front door.

When he reaches the street he stops and stares at the glass and steel buildings rising over the gothic architecture that once covered all of Munich. Once, he did not think he would live to see the future, but now that he has, he is angry that he is unable to explain how he got here to this place, a world he does not, cannot, will not recognise.

He buys lunch in a café down the street. As he walks back to the apartment, a woman leaves the building and hails a cab. He dodges through the crowd, runs, his body slower than it used to be. He bumps into a man older than himself, but does not beg for pardon; he is too intent on the vehicle ahead of him. As he reaches it, it pulls away. All he can see is the back of her head. He stands on the curb, breathing so hard he wonders if he will ever be able to breathe normally again. The bag is heavy in his hands.

Finally, he goes inside. The walk up the stairs is torture. His muscles ache even from that small exertion. He is not in the physical condition he thought he was in. He has spent too much time in his chair, remembering the days when he could take a flight of steps four at a time, instead of doing the work. Perhaps, since his afternoon is now free, he will begin his regimen all over again.

He opens the door. She is still sitting in her chair. For a moment, he merely stares at the back of her head. Grey strands mix with brown on her head. She is not young, and not old, and despite his fevered imagination, she has waited for him.

'It took you a long time,' she says.

He wants to say: I am glad you stayed. I thought I saw you get into a cab. No one stays around me. Thank you for waiting, for being willing to listen. *Instead he says: 'They did not have what I wanted. I had to go to the next restaurant down.'*

TWENTY-SEVEN

Fritz returned to his building at eight o'clock that night, hungry, exhausted, anxious. Despite the Chief's warning, Fritz had stopped at Hitler's apartment again only to find Frau Reichert there alone with her ailing mother. She would not let him see her mother. She said she had not seen Hitler since the weekend, and swore that her mother had not either. Then she begged Fritz not to return again.

He made no promises.

But he went home after that. The meeting with the Chief had left him unsettled, and his inability to find Hitler without the help of the Political Police unsettled him even more. So much so that he failed to note the darkness in the hallway around his apartment until too late.

He pulled his key from his pocket, and fumbled in the dark, cursing the landlord's inability to keep the building up, when a hand covered his.

'Please, Inspector, just a moment.'

The voice was male and familiar, but Fritz couldn't place it. The man standing close to him smelled of sweat and cigarette smoke. Fritz pulled his hand away and put the key back into his pocket.

'Not here,' the man said. 'Inside, perhaps?'

'No,' Fritz said. 'There is a beer hall on the corner. We will meet there in five minutes.'

'It's too public,' the man said. 'Inside would be better.'

'You may either speak to me in the beer hall or on the street. I would like to be able to see your face.'

'What I have to say to you is not for anyone else to hear. Please, Inspector. Hear me.'

'Then tell me why you put out the lights in the hallway.'

The man reached up and screwed the lightbulb back in. The sudden light made Fritz blink. The hallway was empty except for the both of them.

'I don't want to be seen talking with you,' the man said. 'It could get me killed.'

Fritz recognised him. The man still wore his suit, but it had rumpled with use. His wire-rimmed glasses made his eyes look owlish, a feature enhanced by his balding head. He had been the man Fritz had seen outside Hitler's office in the Brown House that morning.

The man was not carrying a weapon, and the fear radiating from his body was palpable.

Fritz fumbled for his key, unlocked the door, and let the man inside. Then Fritz followed and locked the door behind them. He closed the curtains over the window before turning on the light inside. The man hovered near the door, his thumbs hooked on the pockets of his suit coat, marring its line.

'Thank you,' he said.

The man made no comment about the meagreness of the surroundings. Fritz folded the newspaper he had left open on the couch, and tossed his coat over his duffel. Then he went into the small kitchen and cut himself a slice of bread, offering the man a piece by waving his hand. The man shook his head.

'I am Otto Strasser,' the man said.

So the young Brownshirt had been right. A Strasser had been in the Brown House. Only it was the wrong brother.

'I would like to talk about Geli Raubal,' Otto said.

'I know no other reason you would be here.' Fritz took a bite of the bread. It was doughy and its crust had been baked with butter. He did not offer Strasser a seat. The man's presence bothered him. It made him think of Hess, and Hess's odd honesty. Otto Strasser was devious enough, Herr Schwarz had said, to plot against Hitler. Perhaps not for Strasser's gain, but for his brother's.

'Why didn't you talk to me this morning?' Fritz asked.

'I didn't know who you were then.'

Fritz brushed some crumbs off his own coat. 'You did well to find me so easily tonight.'

Strasser shrugged. 'I have sources, Inspector. Your home is not secret.'

'Your visit probably is not either.'

'I realise that.' Strasser spoke softly. 'But I have some information you might need to know. I doubt anyone else might have it.'

Fritz took another bite of the bread, and leaned against the counter. 'Were you at Prinzregentenplaz when Geli died?'

'No,' Strasser said. 'I was in Berlin. I came here as soon as I heard.'

'I thought you were no longer a member of the NSDAP.'

'I am no longer a member of *Hitler's* NSDAP.'

'So you came to help your brother regain leadership of the party.' Fritz finished the slice of bread. It would hold him until Strasser left.

'I don't think they realise the extent of the crisis at the Brown House yet,' Strasser said.

'And you do.'

He nodded. 'I know who killed Geli.'

'All the way from Berlin, you got this knowledge?'

'No,' Strasser said. 'Please, Inspector. I know what Hitler was doing to her. It was only a matter of time.'

Despite himself, Fritz was interested. He opened his hand toward the couch. Strasser nodded, loosened his tie, and sat as if he had visited a hundred times before. Fritz remained in the kitchenette, leaning against the counter.

'All right,' Fritz said. 'I'll listen.'

'I liked Geli,' Strasser said. 'I really did. She was a beautiful girl, and so lively. That she is dead —' his voice broke '— that she is dead is a crime against life itself. She would never kill herself. Never.'

'If you are accusing someone of killing her, you will need to be more explicit, Herr Strasser.'

Strasser looked down and nodded. His hands, resting on his knees, fidgeted with the legs of his trousers. 'I took Geli to the Mardi Gras dance last year.'

'I thought Hitler didn't allow her to see anyone.'

'He didn't, usually, but he and I were having difficulties and he wanted to patch them up. Besides, Geli was keen to go, and he couldn't take her. So he let me.' He looked up, his eyes softening with the memory. 'She was giddy with excitement. She would joke with me that I could drive her anyway and Hitler would not know. She drank a lot of champagne and instead of taking my car back to the apartment we walked through the English Garden. The air seemed to sober her up, and by the time we reached the Chinese Tower she clutched my arm and begged me to stop walking.'

Fritz studied Strasser closely. The man spoke softly and occasionally made eye contact, but mostly he gazed at a point to his left. Fritz had seen the technique before, mostly with witnesses trying to recall moments exactly.

'Her wrap had slipped off her shoulder, and she had a whip mark on her shoulder blade. I remarked on it as I brought the wrap up to cover her skin, and she started to cry.'

Fritz had taken women to the Chinese Tower late at night in Mardi Gras. A woman's wrap did not slip without help. But he was not going to interrupt the flow of Strasser's story.

'She said she didn't want to go back. She said her uncle Alfie was a monster and she was afraid of him.'

Strasser stopped. Fritz waited, but when it appeared that Strasser wasn't going to say any more, Fritz asked, 'Did she say why she was afraid of him?'

Strasser nodded. He brought his right hand up and stroked his chin, covering his mouth as he did so, as if to keep the words inside. 'She said… she said the whip wasn't the worst of it. She was crying. She told me things I…' Strasser shook his head. His fingers were over his lips. '…Things I knew only from college. Did you ever read Krafft-Ebing? *Psychopathia Sexualis?*'

'I didn't go to college,' Fritz said, even though he had seen the book.

'God,' Strasser said. He stood and paced to the window, staring at the curtains as if he could see the street below. 'This is going to be more difficult than I thought.'

Fritz waited silently, neither encouraging nor discouraging. He wished he had eaten another slice of bread. His stomach was growling.

Strasser continued to look at the curtains. He clasped his hands behind his back. 'She said she couldn't go back, that when she did, he would make her take off all her clothes and squat over him while he looked at her. Then he would… she would… he wanted her to… every night…' Strasser leaned his head against the window frame. His voice was barely audible. 'He wanted her to… to piss on him… and she would, and that would start it all.' He shook his head, still pressing it against the wall. 'She asked me to get her away from him. She said it was getting worse. He was thinking of more things, other things…'

He sighed and stood. The frame had left a small red mark on his forehead. He shook his head again, his cheeks flushed and eyes a bit too bright.

'God help me, I was so disgusted. I took her home.'

Fritz didn't move. He felt as if his own body were made of glass. Finally, he said, 'Just because a man has unusual sexual practices does not mean he is a killer.'

'My God, man,' Strasser said. 'She was *afraid* of him.'

'But you took her back there,' Fritz said. 'She couldn't have been that afraid.'

'She was afraid,' Strasser said.

Fritz crossed his arms over his chest. 'Let me see if I understand this. You take a girl to the English Garden during Mardi Gras, get her drunk, and then kiss her. While you slide her dress off her shoulder, she winces when you touch a bruise on her shoulder blade. Then she tells you that she is sleeping with her uncle, a man you are having a conflict with, and that his sexual practices are so onerous that you need to rescue her?'

The flush in Strasser's cheeks grew deeper.

'And you expect me to believe this story because you have come to me of your own free will, all the way from Berlin. I should ignore the story in the *Münchner Post* that says your brother will lead the NSDAP, the party you were thrown out of a few short months after you "dated" Geli, and I should forget that you have disliked Hitler from the day you met him. I should also forget that you run political newspapers in Berlin and understand how important information is, especially in the right hands. I should forget that Hitler's people are hinting that his enemies killed his niece to discredit him, and yet you come in here, to talk to me, to discredit Hitler.'

'I am telling you the truth,' Strasser said.

'Perhaps you are,' Fritz said. 'But you have failed to connect Hitler's undinism with your accusation of murder. It would seem to me, if the man is having sexual relations with the woman, that he would want her to live, especially if those relations call for participation.'

'She was afraid of him,' Strasser said.

'A year and a half ago. Yet she continued to live with him, and you did nothing. If you were so convinced Hitler was going to kill her, why didn't you help her get out? Her story of his appetites might have helped win the party back to you.'

'He killed her,' Strasser said.

'Did he?' Fritz asked. 'He was in Nuremberg at the time.'

'Are you so certain? Nuremberg isn't that far away.' Strasser pulled a handkerchief from his pocket and wiped his forehead. 'Hitler's people lie for him. They do it very well.'

'If you have evidence that Hitler killed Geli, bring it to me and I will see that justice will be done.'

Strasser smiled. The look was cold and bitter. 'Justice? Then you will have to pay Franz Gürtner a higher bribe than NSDAP does.'

'If you believe that I will have such trouble convicting Hitler of any crime, why did you come to me?'

'Because the fact that you were conducting an investigation at all gave me hope.' Strasser tightened his tie and clicked his heels together in the Brownshirt manner. 'I can see now that my hope was misplaced. Good night to you, sir.'

He went to the door and let himself out. Fritz waited a moment, half expecting Strasser to return with another story, another way to discredit Hitler. But he did not. Fritz locked the door and cooked himself dinner, before lying on his couch and dreaming of a beautiful brunette with a broken nose begging for his help.

TWENTY-EIGHT

'*Why didn't you believe Strasser?*' she asks.

Fritz's hands are shaking. He has never said such things to a woman before, in any circumstance.

'I believed his story. I did not believe his conclusions. I thought that a man who robs a house will probably not burn it. Sitting here forty years later, it is easy to draw links. Yes, Hitler was a man who had a quick temper, who beat women, who misused them sexually, a man who ordered an entire race of people to their deaths, who approved all sorts of experiments, who sacrificed millions of lives for his ambitions. I know that now. You listen to this, knowing that . It makes a difference.'

'But?' she asks.

'But I did not know it then. He was a politician whose power was growing. He was not unlike so many others. We had no crystal balls. We did not know the kind of power he would gain.'

'So I don't understand,' she says. 'You didn't believe Strasser because you liked Hitler?'

'No,' Fritz says. 'I did not like Hitler. Nor did I like Ernst Thälmann, the Communist, or even Hindenburg himself. I was not a political man. I still am not. I do not see other men as the answers

199

to our problems. I see them as a reflection of who we are, and who we were. In 1931, we were not a nice people.'

'But Strasser,' she says again. She clearly found his argument compelling.

Fritz nods. Perhaps if he knew then what he knows now, he would have found Strasser's argument equally compelling.

'Strasser created many problems for me,' Fritz says. 'He was a well-known critic of Hitler. I also thought Strasser might have killed her to discredit Hitler and to put his own brother in power. What better way to do that than to have Hitler arrested for murder?'

'But he said that Hitler beat the girl and her body did have whip marks when you found it.'

Fritz reaches for a cigarette. 'And most of the NSDAP carried small whips with their uniforms. No one as yet had seen Hitler hit the girl. And all I had was one jealous man who claimed to have dated the girl, and that she told him that Hitler treated her badly.'

The girl grips the edge of her notebook. Her knuckles are turning white. 'What about the paintings?'

'What about them?'

'Don't they show Hitler's unnatural relationship with his niece?'

'Half-niece,' Fritz says. 'No one denied that he loved her. And the paintings, while explicit, showed nothing unnatural. In fact her body had no marks on it at all. I had enough information to confuse me, and nothing more.'

'But you believed Eva Braun.'

'I believed what she did not say.' His smile is small, his stomach tight with tension. 'Forgive me, but in those days it was not so unusual for a man to hit a woman.'

She pulls the notebook closer to her stomach as if protecting it.

'What of the physical evidence? You have said nothing about it.'

He shrugs. 'Because there is little to tell. This case, unfortunately, was not Demmelmayer. It could not be solved with science. There was no gun. The fingerprints in the room were also from Geli, Hitler, Frau Winter, and Frau Reichert, and on the door were Max Amann's as well as Rudolph Hess's.'

'But Hess never said he was there.'

Fritz smiles. She is at last seeing some things on her own.

'No,' he says, 'but I knew he was there. I knew from the beginning there was a third man, and I knew it had to be a Brownshirt. When he was with the body, it became clear that Hess had been in the apartment that morning.'

The girl frowns, her fingers pulling at the spiral wire binding the notebook. 'It seems to me that if Hitler's prints were on the gun, then you have a case.'

'And Frau Winter's, and Geli's. Remember we had an official suicide. So far nothing unusual in that.' Then he smiles at her, taking pity on her frustration. He had felt the same. 'No gun, no suspect, and a lot of motives. It would have been easier for all of us if her death had remained a suicide.'

TWENTY-NINE

Fritz awoke to a loud pounding. His right arm, draped over his eyes, was asleep, and he had a cramp in his neck. Sunlight had turned the curtains opaque, making the lamps which were still on seem like ineffective competition. The pounding resounded again. He sat up, blinked, and ran his left hand through his hair. The remains of last night's dinner still sat on the table, and the room was too hot. His shirt clung to his slightly damp body.

He got up, staggered across the room, and peered through the spyhole in the door. The man waiting in the hall was of medium height with a hawk nose and downward sloping eyes. Frown lines had formed around his mouth, making him appear unhappy, even with his face at rest.

Fritz had never seen the man before.

'What do you want?' Fritz asked.

'I am from NSDAP. I would like to see Detective Inspector Stecher.'

'You may come to the precinct and do that later this morning.'

'I was at the precinct. I understand the Inspector is on

holiday. I would like to talk to him about the way he spends his free time.'

Fritz tucked his shirt into his pants. 'And who are you with the NSDAP?'

'I am the party publisher.'

Max Amann. One of the men who sent Geli's body to Austria. Fritz pulled the door open. 'You have five minutes.'

'I would hope that I don't have to spend them in the hall.'

Fritz nodded and extended a hand. Amann came inside. Fritz closed the door behind him.

'Inspector, I understand that you are conducting an investigation into the death of Geli Raubal.' Amann walked to the centre of the room. He paused over the dirty dishes on the table, glanced at the rumpled cushions on the couch, and conveyed his disgust through his unwillingness to touch anything in the room.

'It's procedure,' Fritz said.

'Nonsense,' Amann said. 'We both know that the Kripo likes to harass the NSDAP. I'm sure that the Minister of Justice would love to know that a case he closed has been reopened by a lower division.'

'The Kripo was called to the scene. The case was closed before we had a chance to complete the paperwork. I am merely trying to fill the file.'

Amann raised his eyebrows. 'On your off time?'

Fritz said nothing. He took a glass from the cupboard and poured himself a drink of water from the tap.

'Just between us, Inspector, let me know why you are hounding the NSDAP.'

'Interesting choice of words, Herr Amann. "Hounding".
I would have nothing to do if you had left the poor girl's
body in her room, and allowed the Kripo to complete
its paperwork.'

'I am sure you would have found something,' Amann said.

'Not if she committed suicide.' Fritz downed the glass of
water, then wiped his mouth with the back of his arm.

'Do you doubt the Minister of Justice's ruling?'

'I am curious as to whether or not he had all the facts.'

'Such as?'

'How the girl's nose got broken. Why the gun she was
holding disappeared. Simple questions. Obvious ones.'

'Are you implying that someone killed her?'

'No.' Fritz set his glass on the counter. 'I am merely curious,
that's all. Perhaps if you tell me your story, I might understand
all of this. I understand you and two of your companions took
the body to Dr Zehrt for a cursory autopsy, and then had it
sent out of the country. I am curious how, between the time
Frau Winter called the Kripo and Dr Zehrt viewed the body,
the Minister of Justice was able to look and determine the
poor girl killed herself.'

Amann tugged on the lapels of his suit coat. His clothing
had a military crispness. Even the tug did not dislodge the
lines of his suit. 'I would be happy to tell you, Inspector. It
was clear to all of us that she had killed herself. Frau
Reichert called me when she could not get Geli's door
open. I left a meeting with two of my companions, and
when we arrived, we found Geli's door locked. We tried to
contact Frau Winter for a key, but we could not reach her,

205

so we kicked in the door. Geli was inside, with the gun in her hand. Suicide. Even her window was closed. The meeting with Dr Zehrt was a mere formality so that we could send the body to Austria.'

'And the gun?' Fritz asked. 'Where is it?'

'We left it in her room.'

'It was gone when I arrived.'

'Perhaps it was back in the gun cabinet. Frau Winter is efficient.'

'The gun is missing,' Fritz said.

Herr Amann shrugged, as if that did not concern him. 'It was there when we removed the body.'

Fritz crossed his arms. 'If she committed suicide, why the cover-up?'

'Cover-up is such a strong word, Inspector. There was no cover-up. There is potential embarrassment for our leader. We thought it best to keep the story from the papers.'

Fritz swept his hand toward the papers on the floor. 'And that didn't work, did it?'

Amann didn't even glance at them. He shrugged instead. 'There are no photographs. No one has seen our grieving Führer. It is better this way.'

'All the innuendo about murder is better than a clear-cut case of suicide?'

'I don't expect you to understand, Inspector.' Amann tugged the sleeves of his shirt so that they extended a half-inch from the sleeves of his coat. Diamond cufflinks gleamed in the faint light. 'There would be innuendo, anyway. The press does not like to believe the NSDAP, even with evidence. So it is better to keep the most sensational aspects of the death away from them. That means no photographs, no chance to look at the Führer's home, no chance to gawk at his life.'

'Ah, yes,' Fritz said. 'Herr Hitler. Where is he? He seems to have become a ghostly figure in all of this.'

'He is shattered by grief.' Amann said the sentence so matter-of-factly that Fritz had to pause before understanding what he had heard.

'Geli was the most important person in his life.'

Amann smiled. 'Now you understand. Yes, indeed. He would do nothing to hurt her. He wanted everything for her.'

Nothing to hurt her. A denial where none was required. 'And yet you send her body to a country where Herr Hitler is not allowed, so that he cannot even attend the funeral.'

'He was too distraught to travel.'

'You knew that when you put the body on the train?'

'Of course,' Amann said.

'But Hitler hadn't even come back from Nuremberg yet.'

'I spoke with his chauffeur by telephone. We have come into the twentieth century, you know, Inspector.'

'I saw Hitler on Saturday night,' Fritz said. 'He looked as if he could travel.'

Amann smiled a slight, small smile that deepened his frown lines. 'You do not know him. He was probably startled to see you, since the case was closed.'

'I need to speak with him, Herr Amann. Where is he?'

'You have no reason to see the Führer, Inspector. The girl is buried and you can do nothing to change the Minister's ruling.'

'You have not heard me,' Fritz said. 'I do not want to change the Minister's ruling. I merely want to have a complete file on the case.'

'You will have to complete your file without the Führer. In fact, I would call the file complete now.'

Fritz raised his chin so that he looked down his nose at Amann. 'That sounds strangely like a threat, Herr Amann.'

'It is no threat,' Amann said. 'It is advice.'

'What are you afraid of?' Fritz asked. 'Closing my files should not bother you if all is as you say.'

'The NSDAP is not popular with the authorities. Perhaps your report could be compromised.'

Fritz shook his head. 'I have a reputation to consider, Herr Amann. I do not make accusations without evidence.'

Amann's eyebrows furrowed. 'And whom would you accuse?'

'No one. Is there someone I should be looking for?'

They stared at each other for a moment. Finally, Amann said, 'You realise that the Führer has many enemies.'

'I am learning that life in the rarefied strata of the NSDAP is not all glory.'

'We cannot let them think they could be successful in intimidating any part of the NSDAP.'

'And you don't think they feel successful just in your denials. If Geli was murdered, you are besmirching her reputation by claiming she killed herself. You are hurting your own party by saying a woman who lived with your Führer is so unhappy she has to kill herself.'

'We don't want an investigation.' Amann said.

'I believe an investigation is the least of your worries,' Fritz said.

'Now it is my turn to think you are threatening me.'

'No threat,' Fritz said. 'Look at it outside the panic for a moment. Hitler was in Nuremberg. He was not involved. You might gain sympathy for your cause by claiming that Geli Raubal was murdered by rivals.'

'It would show them that our security can be breached.'

'I would think,' Fritz said slowly, 'they know that already.'

Amann swallowed. He pursed his lips and tugged at his lapels again.

Fritz let his arms fall to his side. 'Let me see Hitler. Let me find out whom he believes could do such a thing. Then I will close the files, and if the papers want evidence, they can use mine.'

'The Führer cannot talk to you,' Amann said.

'Why not?' Fritz asked.

'He will not see anyone. He is too shattered. We don't –' Amann stopped himself, swallowed, then tried again. 'We don't know if he will continue to head the party.'

Fritz suddenly felt lightheaded. 'Are you saying he is no longer competent to lead?'

'She is the love of his life, Inspector. He cannot even tolerate visitors. I don't know how he can go into public.'

They also discussed who, if something were to happen, should be Hitler's successor. Gregor Strasser was named... Fritz licked his dry lips. 'How long will you wait for Hitler to heal?'

'As long as we have to,' Amann said. 'He is our vision.'

Fritz nodded.

'So you see,' Amann continued, 'why we can't have anything disturb him. We need him well. Time is short.'

'Yes,' Fritz said. 'Time is very short.' And getting shorter.

★

'It seems odd,' she says, 'that he would come to you.'

Fritz smiles. He can still see Max Amann's face, the fire in his eyes when he spoke of his Führer. 'It is not odd,' Fritz says. 'They had already spoken to the Chief Inspector. That hadn't worked. I was getting close, and they were frightened.'

'Did he really think he could scare you away?'

'Oh, yes.' Fritz sighs and leans back in his chair. 'But I had seen so much, nothing frightened me.'

'You were not afraid then?'

He shakes his head.

'But you are afraid now?'

He doesn't look at her. 'The memory, it brings with it the knowledge of the later years, of what happened to men like me when Hitler came to power.'

'What happened?' she asks.

'They died,' he says.

210

THIRTY

When Max Amann left, Fritz went to the precinct to use the hated telephone. He had little time, so he used it as wisely as he could. He called Berlin, spoke to the newspaper office where Otto Strasser worked, and discovered that Strasser spoke the truth, that he had come to Munich after hearing of Geli's death.

Or, at least, he had set up his alibi before he left.

Fritz had too much to do. He needed Henrich. He found him going over a witness list.

'I need you to go to Berlin,' Fritz said. 'You must check Otto Strasser's alibi, then check on his followers.'

'What of Gregor?' Henrich asked.

Fritz nodded. 'Check on him when you return.'

'What will you be doing?' Henrich asked.

'Following my only other lead,' Fritz said.

★

'Otto Strasser seems too important for you to have given him to Henrich,' she says.

Fritz smiles. 'Otto Strasser was obvious,' he says, 'and many people discussed him. What I found important were the silences, the things not said.'

'The denials,' she says.

'And the denials, where none were needed.'

✳

The drive to Nuremberg took two hours. Fritz timed it, deliberately going slow, then adding fifteen minutes to the total time. Hitler's story, sent to the Kripo through his agents while Fritz was in Vienna, was that he had heard about Geli's death on Saturday morning, and had hurried back so quickly that he had got a speeding ticket in Ebenhausen on the way back. Fritz had seen the ticket. It was issued on Saturday morning, after Geli's body had been taken to Dr Zehrt.

No one would talk about Hitler's role in all of this. His chauffeur, the only other person who knew Hitler's exact schedule, had disappeared as well.

✳

'So by this time, you believed Hitler killed her?'

Fritz shakes his head. He does not want to give that impression. 'I suspected someone in NSDAP, but I did not know who. I had nothing clear, no real reason for anyone to kill the girl.'

'Except Eva.'

'Not even Eva. She had no real way in.'

'I don't understand why you didn't investigate those who hated him — the Communists, maybe.'

He likes it better when she is silent. But as he gets deeper into the story, she is silent less and less. 'It was clear from the first that Geli died at the hands of NSDAP, and not any other way.'

212

She holds up one hand, then stops the tape and turns it over. As she presses 'record', she says, 'It is not clear to me.'

'A political murder, especially of a young and beautiful girl, would have helped the NSDAP. Had they been thinking clearly, they would have played it that way from the beginning. But something caused them to panic.'

'A suicide, perhaps?'

'With a broken nose?'

'The nose could have happened in a different incident.'

Fritz nods. 'It could have. But it didn't. I did not make those kinds of mistakes ever in my career. And you forget Father Pant.'

'He was not the expert. You were.'

'Yes, and I saw a murder victim.'

'So someone in the NSDAP knew who killed her, and hid it.'

'Ineffectively.'

'But why kill a 23-year-old girl who had no interest in politics?'

Fritz shrugs. 'A hundred reasons. To frighten Hitler. To get him to resign.'

'That would be the Strassers.'

Fritz nods. 'Or perhaps she knew something she wasn't supposed to. She went on many important dinners with Hitler.'

'What about the paintings?'

'The paintings suggest blackmail, but who was blackmailing whom?'

'Hitler's sexual practices might have created attention.'

'No.' Fritz picks up his pack of cigarettes. 'No, there you are wrong.'

She frowns. 'Wouldn't the German people be shocked at what he was doing with his own unmarried niece?'

'No.' Fritz puts a cigarette in his mouth, grabs his lighter, and flicks the edge. The flame soars, leaving a butane stench in the air.

'Come now,' The girl says. 'The Germans come from the same Western traditions as the rest of us. You can't tell me that they were so liberal as to tolerate that kind of behaviour.'

'It is not liberal.' Fritz inhales, letting the tobacco cool his throat. He exhales in a big puff of white. 'We all did things in those days, things we were not proud of. There were live sex shows in Berlin in the Twenties. Good women sold their bodies for bread in the Great Inflation. We did not talk about our private behaviour. If we pointed the finger at one man, we might have to point it at ourselves.'

She studies him for a long time, long enough for him to smoke the entire cigarette and stub the butt in the cut-glass ashtray. 'You never explored the sexual evidence, did you? You never asked those questions. You let that information go right past you. I bet you never knew who sent you the paintings.'

'It wasn't important.'

'It was important enough to tell me.'

'It goes to motivation.'

'Motivation?' She clicks the top of her pen. 'You solved the case then.'

'You doubted that?' He wonders if he should be offended. Perhaps he is offended too much.

'You've been so cryptic, and then you retired after this case was closed. The more I listen to you, the more I know you are not the kind of man who would take money to remain silent. I thought perhaps you retired in disgrace.'

'Perhaps I retired because I could no longer make money in my

214

profession. There was a point when the city of Munich could not pay its employees.'

'And a point when the banks closed. You don't strike me as the kind of man who would leave then. It would give you even less security.' Then she blinks. 'Something robbed you of your security?'

Fritz removes another cigarette from his pack. 'Long before this,' he says. 'Long before this.'

THIRTY-ONE

He drove to the door of the Deutscher Hof hotel, and sat outside it for a long time before going in. The hotel was nice, but not extravagant, the sort of place a well-known man would stop for a short night. Again, Fritz checked his pocket watch. Two hours. No one had said if Hitler had business in Nuremberg. He would have arrived a little after three in the afternoon, too early to retire for the evening. If Fritz had been driving and planning to make a speech in Hamburg the following night, he would have stopped farther from Munich – Kassel perhaps, which was at least half way. The last thing Fritz would have done was leave the bulk of the driving for the day of the speech.

He got out of the car and walked under the awning to the interior of the hotel. It smelled of mildew and dust, the cumulative effect being one of age, even though the furnishings looked new. The clerk behind the counter was a bespectacled man whose dark hair was slicked back and who filled his moments with movement so that he looked important.

Fritz waited until the foyer was clear before approaching

the desk. 'I am looking for the clerk who was on duty Friday afternoon.'

The man looked up. He was younger than Fritz had expected, in his early twenties, and poor. The cuffs of his white shirt were frayed. 'I was.'

'Were you also working on Saturday morning?'

'No, sir. That would have been Erich.'

'And is Erich here today?'

'No, sir. May I help you with something, sir?'

Fritz nodded. He pulled his papers from his pocket, then leaned across the desk. 'I am Detective Inspector Stecher of the Munich Kripo. I would like to know if you remember a man registering on Friday afternoon.'

'Many men registered on Friday. Have you a photograph?'

'No.' Fritz scanned the foyer. No one had entered. 'Adolf Hitler, the head of NSDAP stayed here Friday night.'

The clerk swallowed and slicked back his already perfect hair. 'We're not allowed to talk about the guests, sir.'

'I don't want to know about him,' Fritz said. 'I would just like to know what time he arrived.'

The clerk nodded. He reached for the registry book beside him, opened it, and flipped to Friday's page. 'I have his man coming in here at 7 p.m., sir. I don't remember him. I do know that I never saw Herr Hitler. He let his man do all the work.'

'Seven p.m.?' Fritz asked. 'May I see your record?'

'Certainly.' The clerk spun the book around. 'We have it twice, sir. See where the name is listed? Then we make a notation for the possession of the key. Erich recorded it returned at 10 a.m. the following morning.'

'You never saw Herr Hitler?'

The clerk shook his head. 'And I wanted to. We don't get well-known Bavarians here much.'

'Would it have been possible for Herr Hitler to have checked in that afternoon?'

'Not without a record, sir. And I do remember that afternoon. We had no rooms at all until five. It was causing problems with some of the other guests.'

Fritz took a deep breath. 'I see. Do you have a record of incoming phone calls as well?'

'Yes, sir.'

'And do you have one for Herr Hitler on Saturday morning?'

The clerk spun the book back toward him. He ran a hand down the page, then took out another book and ran through that. 'None, sir. We had no calls for guests all day.'

Hess had said that he had contacted Hitler before Hitler left for Hamburg. Hitler's official story claimed that someone had called the hotel, but Hitler had already left, so the hotel's dispatch motorcycle courier had overtaken Hitler's car.

'Who is your motorcycle courier?' Fritz asked.

The clerk smiled as if Fritz had made a joke. 'We use one of the services, Inspector. We have no courier of our own.'

'Are the services open on Saturday?'

'I believe they are, sir, but again, we have no record of anyone contacting them.'

'You rely heavily on records,' Fritz said. 'Does everyone?'

The clerk nodded. 'Keeping track of the day-to-day

dealings is part of my job. If I fail to note a transaction or a phone call, it is grounds for dismissal.'

Fritz said nothing, although he had a sudden picture of the tedium of the clerk's job, and the tyranny of a small-minded master.

'So tell me,' Fritz said. 'If a man arrived early to this hotel on Friday, left on Saturday, also early, and then received a phone call, what would happen?'

'If someone arrived early, we would have done our best to accommodate, but he would have been told to wait. His arrival would have been noted, and the time he was put into a room noted as well. Then his departure and payment would have been recorded, as would any phone call that came after he left.'

'And how would you have forwarded a message if the phone call was an emergency?'

The clerk shrugged. 'We have never faced that situation. I suppose we would have tried to contact the person at his next stop, if we knew it.'

Fritz nodded. 'When will Erich be back?'

'He works only the weekend, sir. We won't see him until Saturday.'

Fritz thanked the clerk for his time, and then left. Outside, he sat in his car and stared at the hotel. He would probably return on the weekend, to see if Erich confirmed the clerk's story, but Fritz really had no doubt that he would. The Hitler camp had lied again, this time about Hitler's whereabouts, and Fritz didn't like where this was going.

'So Hitler killed her.'

'There was no proof of that,' Fritz says. 'Only discrepancies in a story filled with them. It really didn't matter what time Hitler got to the hotel, if the girl died during the night as they claimed. He was still out of the way. The phone call the next morning, though, that had me baffled. I wasn't certain why they lied about that.'

She shakes her head, looks at him, her perplexity showing on her face. 'I don't understand. If everyone lies and the physical evidence is unimportant, how do you get at the truth?'

'You hope you find someone who will not lie,' he says. 'Or you hope you can bluff your way to getting someone to confess.'

THIRTY-TWO

By the time he returned to Munich, it was late. He had timed the drive again, and again it had come out to two hours, subtracting the time he spent in Ebenhausen. The traffic police did have a record of the ticket given to Hitler's Mercedes, but no one in the office remembered the man driving, or if he had a passenger.

Fritz drove by the coroner's office, and swung the car through the narrow alley between the buildings. The alley had once been a road, but it was barely big enough for an automobile, so it had became an alley in recent years. Zehrt used it for his coroner's wagon, and often kept the road blocked. It was not blocked tonight.

Fritz stopped his car near the rear door. A single light burned in the offices, in the examining room. Through the unshaded window, Zehrt worked over a corpse, alone.

The Schupo had spoken to Zehrt about his unwillingness to cover the windows, saying it was both a breach of security and a danger for the coroner himself. But Zehrt had merely laughed. He claimed that only those with the strongest stomachs could watch him cut open a corpse, and he also maintained that it took an even stronger man to break into a place with a dead body already on the table.

The years had proven him correct.

Fritz, however, had watched many an autopsy. His stomach was not as strong as Zehrt's, but it was close.

Fritz got out of the car, and walked to the window. His feet crunched on the small parking space. Grass had grown over cobblestones so brittle that they had broken into tiny rocks. Still Zehrt did not look up. He was intent on the corpse in front of him, a beefy, balding man with a tattoo on his right forearm. Zehrt was examining the tattoo when Fritz rapped on the window.

Zehrt looked up slowly, as if people knocked on his window every night. He shook his head when he saw Fritz, but Fritz knocked again. Finally Zehrt set his tools down, pulled off his gloves, and came to the window. He yanked it open. The odours of formaldehyde and death surrounded him.

'I am in the middle of work,' he snapped.

'I have a few questions. It will only take a moment.'

'I don't have a moment,' Zehrt said.

'Looks like you have a Communist on the table.'

'I don't know what he is. He was knifed in the English Garden, but the wounds seem superficial. I am beginning to wonder if his heart went with the fear and shock.'

Fritz shrugged. 'If anyone could tell it would be you.'

Zehrt stared at him. 'You aren't going to go away, are you?'

Fritz shook his head.

'All right, then. Come in.' He closed the window so quickly that Fritz had to step away from it. Fritz went to the

224

wide wooden door in the back. The bolts clicked as Zehrt unlocked the door, and pulled Fritz inside. Then he slammed the door shut.

'I didn't want to be seen talking to you,' Zehrt said. The odour of formaldehyde was so strong it almost made Fritz sneeze.

'Do you work for the NSDAP now?'

'No,' Zehrt said. The light from the examining room filtered into this small hallway. Tables and cabinets lined the walls. Zehrt had not turned on any other lights.

'Then they have something on you. Tell me, Gerhart. I will get them away from you.'

Zehrt shook his head. 'It is not worth the Kripo's time. Just ask your question and get out.'

'Two questions,' Fritz said. He was not willing to let the blackmail go, but it could wait until a later time. 'First, when did you see Geli Raubal's body?'

Zehrt let out a small breath of air. The girl's name seemed to diminish him. 'I am not supposed to talk about the girl.'

'Police reasons or NSDAP?'

'Please, Fritz —'

'Gerhart, I am only going to ask questions that should have been in your report, had there been one.'

'I already told you to see the body for yourself.'

'And I did. I don't want to know how she died. That's obvious. I need to know when they brought the body to you.'

Zehrt rubbed his hands together. 'Saturday morning, just like I told you. You were only a few hours behind them.'

Fritz nodded. He expected that Zehrt wouldn't have been

in the office if he hadn't had a body to tend to. 'I want to know time of death.'

'You know I can't pinpoint that with any kind of accuracy. And it was a cursory exam –'

'Time of death, Gerhart. You can give me that within a few hours just by looking at a body.'

Zehrt put his hand on Fritz's arm. Zehrt was trembling. 'Please, my friend, go. You are angering people you shouldn't anger.'

'And what can they do to me? They aren't even the party in power.'

'They will be, though. They are second in the country right now. Please, Fritz. You don't know these men. I do.'

Fritz shook Zehrt's hand off him, and crossed his arms. 'I won't leave unless you answer my very simple question.'

Zehrt ran his hands over his bloodstained smock. He glanced at the window, then at the body on the table. 'Friday afternoon,' he said. 'She died Friday afternoon.'

THIRTY-THREE

*F*ritz *pauses, takes a breath, then opens a new pack of cigarettes. He is filled with the same elation he felt the moment Zehrt had told him when Geli died. Then, for a brief second, he had believed he would be able to find her killer. But Zehrt had thrown him out, and Fritz realised that he would have to fight fear.*

Others' fear.

He is still fighting fear.

Only now it is his own.

'So,' the girl says, obviously filling the silence. 'He did kill her. But you didn't catch him. Is this why you're telling me all of this? To let me know that you had the power to stop one of the greatest madmen in the history of the world, and you did not?'

The cigarette he is holding snaps in half. Tobacco spills on his lap. He brushes it off to hide his shaking hands.

'What I had was circumstantial,' he says. He takes another cigarette and puts it into his mouth. 'I had only speculation and testimony of eye-witnesses that contradicted it. No one could place him there. No one saw him. I had nothing yet.'

She runs a hand through her long hair. 'But I thought you said you solved this.'

227

'I did.'

'And Hitler did not kill her?'

He sets the pack back on the table and runs his hand over the smooth paper. His fingernails have yellowed over the years from the force of his habit.

'It is not so simple,' he says. 'Why do you always look for it to be simple?'

She stares at him a moment, then sighs. 'I can stay longer if you think we would finish tonight.'

He wants to ask what her hurry is, but then he realises he has probably conveyed a 40-year old sense of urgency. He knew, leaving Zehrt's, that he only had so much time before all the holes were filled, all the cracks were painted over.

He had been like this girl, thinking that once he solved the case, everything would be all right. He too had got lost in the simple answer. He had believed his own press after Demmelmayer, had thought that science was the way of the future, that science would shed a light on the darkness of the human heart.

He was wrong.

He was always wrong.

'We will not finish tonight,' he says. 'Go get yourself a good German dinner. We still have a day or two. That is, if you want to hear the rest.'

'Of course I do,' she says. 'I want to hear how this concluded.'

Concluded. Her words ring as she packs her equipment, tucks her notebook in her bag, and lets herself out the door. Concluded meant conclusions, and he has none. She is still young enough that she does not understand life's inability to resolve. Even when an event ends, its memory lingers and the questions it raises linger as well. Perhaps,

228

if he had not taken the case, things would have been different. Perhaps, if he had asked for help from the start, he might have had a proper investigation. Perhaps, if the Chief had not had a vendetta against the NSDAP, there would have been no case at all.

Fritz waits until he can no longer hear her footsteps on the stairs, then he goes like a man possessed into his bedroom. He flicks on the light. The blanket is rumpled – he slept on top of it the night before and did not straighten it for the first time since the years in London – and a pair of shoes lie toe-to-toe in the middle of the floor. He steps over them and heads for his closet, yanking the cardboard box toward him so hard that it tears. He squats on the floor and pulls the photographs out, placing them around him like still frames from an old movie.

The wedding picture from before the war. Gisela made her dress. Its white simplicity flows around her, half hidden by the flowers she holds, blooms downward. His boutonnière is also upside down, a detail he has forgotten. The suit he wore was his father's, and it was too tight in the shoulders, the sleeves rise showing his wrists. He was young then, barely 21, and he looked 16.

According to the custom of the age, they do not smile, but Gisela's eyes are young and warm.

He cannot look at them.

Nor can he clearly see Wilhelm's christening picture. Or the last picture taken en famille during the war. The photograph of Fritz, formal in his uniform, is dog-eared on the edges. Gisela told him that she used to clutch it in her hand when she slept at night, praying that he would be safe.

Safe.

Prayers.

He had survived at least, but God had never allowed him to be safe.

The last photograph is actually a clipping, one he pasted to a piece of cardboard. The tape is yellow. He cannot look at it either.

She had been so angry, as if it had been his fault that Wilhelm died. She had been with the boy; Fritz had been looking for work, for money, for anything. The family could not survive on the weekly ration of two loaves of bread, 10 ounces of meat, a bit of butter and a bit of jam. They tried to hoard everything, give what they could to Wilhelm, but he did not thrive. Nor did Gisela's garden.

Or her mind.

When they finally moved to the city, after Wilhelm's death, Fritz thought she might improve, she might find something to fill her time while he searched for ways of making money, keeping them fed.

She filled her time.

He gets up, steps over the photographs and goes to the phone in the kitchen. He has the number memorised. This time he waits for an answer. He demands Maria, says he will pay extra for the stockings and properly applied make-up, only he needs her to hurry, can she hurry? He needs her there, right now.

The voice on the other end quotes a price double what he has paid before.

Fritz does not care. He says he will pay in cash if she can arrive within the half hour. Then he hangs up.

While he waits he cleans the apartment, dumps the ashtray, and does the dishes. Gisela hates dirt, always has, complains about it when he tracks it in. He closes the bedroom door because he cannot bring himself to go inside. Something on the floor bothers him. He doesn't need the bedroom. A bedroom is a luxury he has not had much of during his life. She will understand.

230

He takes the money out of the drawer and places it on the tiny key stand beside the door. Then he brushes his hair and tries not to go to the window to see if she is waiting outside.

He hates it when she waits outside.

Finally, there is a knock on the door. The handle goes down, and the door opens. Gisela slips in, her hair and coat dotted with drops of rain.

'Detective?' she asks, her voice small and wrong, just as the word is wrong. For a moment, he sees Maria, and he shakes his head. She is wrong.

'Detective?' she says again.

He puts a finger to his lips. He wants to see her. Gisela, his wife. 'Take off the coat.'

She does, her hands trembling. Her eyes are wide. The kohl makes them dark and foreign, exotic, with no touch of innocence, no happiness at all. Her lips are full and red and her hair, once brown and wrapped around her head like a proper woman's, is clipped to an American bob, held out of her eyes with tiny pins.

She wears a black teddy that comes to the edges of her nipples and lines her bony hips. The weight she lost has not come back, will never come back, and time has ravaged her skin, making it yellow and tough as parchment. Her stockings are crooked, the seam wobbling up the sides of her legs, the garter improperly hooked. Her brown shoes do not match. In her left hand, she holds a riding crop as if she is going to use it.

He takes a step toward her. She cringes against the door. 'Take off the shoes,' he says.

'They're all we had —'

'Quiet!' He cannot stand the voice. He doesn't want to hear the voice.

She pulls off her shoes and drops them beside her.

'Turn around,' he says.

She does, still hunched.

He goes to her, unhooks the stockings, and she squeals in fright, wresting herself away from him. Her garter snaps against her leg, and she squeals again, bringing her hands to protect her head, riding crop forgotten.

'I was only going to fix your stockings,' he says.

She doesn't appear to hear him. She swallows and pushes up against the door so hard her pancake make-up leaves a trail of faint brown powder. 'Please, Detective, please,' she says in that wrong voice. 'The last time I couldn't work for a month and they almost turned me out. Please. I can't do it again. I can't.'

The voice breaks the illusion completely. He was never a detective around her. He became a detective because of her.

'Please,' the woman says again.

He is towering over her, giving her no room to move. Like the last time. After that, he hadn't slept for weeks. He was afraid to. Afraid of the dreams.

Of the memories.

Of the last time he saw Gisela.

Of the last time he saw his wife.

He stayed awake. And then the American came.

He takes the money off the key stand and hands it to the woman, Maria. She stares up at him. The kohl around her eyes has run, leaving black streaks on her face. Her lipstick is smeared, giving her half a clown's grin.

'Get out,' he says.

She does not wait for him to say it twice. She grabs her shoes and her coat, and clutches them to her chest as she runs out the door. He closes the door behind her, listening to the thud of her bare feet on the wooden staircase, hearing the panic in the rapidity of the movement.

He leans his head on the door. He is amazed they sent her back at all.

THIRTY-FOUR

Zehrt's paranoia had infected Fritz. All the way back to his apartment, Fritz checked his mirrors, making certain he wasn't being followed. At times he was the only car on a side street; he knew he was travelling alone.

Still he couldn't shake the sense of unease as he stopped the car in front of his apartment building. The streetlights were bright here, and the sidewalks empty. The shadows were deep, though, near the trees and in the doorways. He paused in the car, checked as best he could, then let himself out.

In the morning he would report Zehrt's terror to the Chief and see if something could be done to prevent the police coroner from being blackmailed by the NSDAP. In the morning, Fritz would also find a safer place for the paintings, and the negatives of Geli's body.

In the morning he would find Frau Dachs and make her talk to him. Now more than ever he was convinced they had kept her from him, that she knew something she shouldn't.

He closed the car door and the sound echoed on the empty street. His heart was pounding. If Zehrt had explained the nature of the blackmail, Fritz wouldn't have been quite as nervous. But Zehrt had left it up to his imagination… and Fritz's imagination was extremely vivid.

He walked around the car, keeping an eye open for any movement in the shadows before him. When he stepped into the pool of light left by the streetlight he heard a scrape behind him. He started to turn –

– as a body crashed into him. Only his preparedness kept him from being knocked off balance. He threw the man off him as another grabbed his side. Fritz stumbled sideways, threw the second man off, only to be hit by a third, and then a fourth.

The first came back for more, as did the second. Fritz punched the man in front of him while elbowing the one beside him and kicking the legs out from under the third. Then Fritz grabbed the fourth and tossed him into a nearby car. The first hit again, catching Fritz in the kidneys and sending pain shooting through his back. He punched the first man hard, brought the second down, and took a deep breath –

– when more men attacked him from the shadows. This time the men were too many to count. He was already winded from the first assault. They were hitting and kicking him, but Fritz fought back, using fists, elbows and feet. One attacker fell to the street, another hit the hood of the car, still another banged into the streetlight and slumped to the ground.

But they kept coming. A fist connected with Fritz's nose, and blood spurted down his face. He was hitting blindly now, not sure how many attackers there were, how many still hiding. It seemed like for each he hit, another appeared. He was being buffeted by the strength of their blows, arms and legs flailing, connecting, being satisfied with each exclamation of pain from the other side.

Then hands clapped him around the ears, making him dizzy. He was choking on blood, its iron taste filling his mouth. He couldn't breathe through his nose. He lashed out with his fists, but hands grabbed his wrists and pulled them together while a booted foot knocked his legs out from underneath him.

He landed hard on the bodies of the men he had felled. The wind left his body in a painful rush. The blood was in his mouth, his eyes, his nose. He couldn't breathe.

Everything became a struggle for one mouthful of air. He rolled off his back, and encountered a foot. More feet – kicking him, his ribs, his back, his legs. He bent his head and pulled his arms around his head, feeling the blows in his shoulders. A metal-toed boot connected with his elbow, sending shooting, shuddering pain down his arm, but the blood was out of his mouth. He was breathing. He was breathing again.

But he couldn't get up. He tried to pull himself toward the curb, but the boots wouldn't let him. No one said anything. All he heard were the thuds and his own grunts of pain. They were all around him. He couldn't get away. He thought of crawling under the car, but he couldn't go in that direction either. The men below him were stirring, knocking him loose, and he fell to the cobblestone, his belly turned toward the kicking feet.

He rolled, lay flat, wishing they would stop, praying they would and suspecting they wouldn't until they kicked him to death. He kept crawling and they kept pushing him back, until he had no more strength. Counter-intuitive, but part of the training: he had no hope, so he pretended to have none. He let his arms drop and his body go flat. When they kicked him, he kept the sounds bottled in his throat. He was beyond pain. Every part of him hurt, he couldn't hurt any more. Blood ran hot and thick from his nose and pooled against his cheek on the cold stone.

The kicking stopped. Still he didn't move. Something clattered on the stone beside him, but he didn't look up to see what it was. The booted feet marched off in a unit – goose-stepped like they did at the Brown House. His eyes were closed. He saw flickering colours against his lids – green, red, sometimes yellow. He knew he should get up, but he didn't want to, not yet. He was sure they would kick him again.

He was cold and the blood had dried on his face. He might have passed out; he didn't know. All he knew was that someone was approaching. He heard a whistle – a tin whistle, Schupo whistle – and then voices, hushed, and frightened. As if they expected to get kicked for approaching him.

'– call a doctor –'

'– Kripoman who lives upstairs –'

'– knew something would happen. Those men were here before dark –'

'– is really famous, you know. Pictures in the papers and –'

'– break into the apartment, ma'am?'

He focused on that voice. It was male. It sounded official.

'Oh, no.' The woman had spoken before. 'I would have called for help if someone suspicious was in the building.'

Thanks, Fritz wanted to say, but he couldn't get his lips to move. It felt as if every part of him was broken.

A car pulled up. He could feel its rumble in the stones beneath him. The men he had landed on were gone. He wondered when they left. He didn't remember them getting up.

The conversation swirled around him, but he concentrated on the car. The door opened and someone wearing boots got out. He cringed at the sound of booted feet on cobblestone.

'Ah, Christ!'

The Chief. The Chief was there. Fritz felt a relief so deep he nearly cried.

'– know this man?'

'Yeah.' The Chief crouched beside him, cherry pipe tobacco mixing with the smell of blood. 'Fritz, can you hear me? Fritz?'

Fritz lifted his right hand off the cobblestone, the pain so great he nearly passed out. He grabbed the Chief's coat. The wool was warm and familiar.

'The apartment,' he said. 'Don't let them go. Guard it. Zehrt warned me.'

'Zehrt is dead,' the Chief said. 'I was coming to tell you. He was hit by a car when he left his office tonight.'

Zehrt dead, and Fritz left for dead. He hadn't got close. He had solved the case. The proof was all in the negative.

They would have left him alone if he hadn't been this close. They wouldn't have killed Zehrt if the time of death weren't important.

They were protecting Hitler.

All along, they had been protecting Hitler.

'What's this?' the Chief said. He picked up something near Fritz's face. Fritz squinted. A bit of silver reflected in the light. He had seen it before. A swastika, once the symbol for the Teutonic Knights, lately co-opted by the Brownshirts. Hitler's men. They had meant the attack as a warning.

But to whom?

THIRTY-FIVE

'*My God,*' she says. *She sits in front of a pile of pastries. She has brought enough to feed them for days. He is glad. It keeps her from commenting on his closed bedroom door, and the obvious fact that he slept in his clothes. 'How badly were you injured?'*

'Three broken ribs, a broken nose, and a cracked elbow. That doesn't count all the missing teeth and the bruises over most of my body.' He grins. 'Imagine how I would have felt if I hadn't been prepared.'

'You would have died.'

He shrugs. 'It was a common way to kill someone in those days. If caught, the defendants could claim the attack merely got out of hand. It also showed no intent.'

'How long were you hospitalised?'

'Overnight,' he says. 'And even that was too long.'

*

Fritz had planned to go to the precinct briefly and then home to recuperate. Each movement was agony. His face had swollen to twice its normal size. His torso was black and blue, and his legs carried the red imprints of steel-toed boots.

241

He wouldn't have stopped at the precinct at all, except that he needed to speak to the Chief. Fritz knew who killed Geli, but not how to prove it. He needed the weight of the Kripo behind him. He needed to find the gun, examine the apartment, talk to Hitler. He couldn't do that without help.

The Chief had to step in. Fritz needed to know if he would. Because, during that long night of pain, Fritz figured out who the warning was for.

It was for the Chief. Fritz was working on the Chief's vendetta. But so far, the Chief was untouchable. They could kill Zehrt and Fritz, but someone would investigate the death of the Chief Inspector. Not even the Minister of Justice could protect them from that.

Fritz made the agonising walk into the precinct. His fellow officers stared at him, and then looked away. Detective Inspector Stecher, who could best any of them in a fight, nearly killed by the NSDAP. It made him human.

It brought him shame.

He stood as tall as he could. He met their eyes, nodded at a few as he walked through the hall. Then he knocked on the Chief Inspector's door and entered without waiting for an answer.

The Chief was at his desk. He looked older, his eyes shadows buried in his face.

'We have a case,' he said.

He was referring to the beatings, to Zehrt's death. The Chief knew as well as Fritz that those actions wouldn't have happened if Fritz hadn't got close.

'We have nothing.' Fritz spit out the words. 'We have

circumstance, we have fear, and we have intimidation. What we do not have is evidence.'

The Chief leaned back. 'Can you continue on the case? If not, Henrich –'

'Henrich is in Berlin.'

'He got back a few hours ago. Strasser's story checks out.'

'I don't need Henrich,' Fritz said. He stood stiffly, pain shooting through his joints. 'I need the full weight of the Kripo behind me. I need the Political Police to find Herr Hitler. I need to conduct this like a real investigation.'

The Chief shook his head. 'I can't do that.'

'Why not?' Fritz snapped. 'Do it under the guise of investigating Zehrt's death.'

'It was ruled accidental.'

'By whom? Gürtner?'

The Chief didn't meet his gaze.

'Goddammit!' Fritz slammed his hands on the desk, ignoring the pain. 'All the more reason.'

'I cannot run a full investigation without evidence,' the Chief said. 'Bring me evidence. Hard evidence, and then we might have a chance.'

'There is no hard evidence,' Fritz said. 'The gun is missing. The body is buried. The apartment has been cleaned and wiped free of fingerprints by now. We will have nothing.'

'There has to be something,' the Chief said. 'Find it. Quickly. There is little time left.'

∗

The girl stops him with a movement of her hand. She looks at him, squints, as if she can see inside him.

'You don't seem well this morning,' she says.

'I didn't sleep much.'

'Obviously.' She pauses, reluctant to say what she has on her mind. 'I want to hear the end of this, but I can wait until you feel better. I can come back this afternoon. Or tomorrow.'

He shakes his head. He is almost done. He needs to finish before the memories overwhelm him completely. 'Don't you want to know what happened?'

'Of course,' she says. 'But not at the expense of your health.'

'My health.' He smiles. 'My health is the least of my worries.'

*

Henrich sat at his desk, typing the last of his report. He looked exhausted, like a man who had been up all night. He smelled like a man who had driven for days and had not bathed.

'You look like hell,' Henrich said.

'So do you,' Fritz said. He tossed Henrich the keys to his own car. 'You drive.'

'Where are we going?' Henrich asked.

'To settle this,' Fritz said.

*

She curses softly, the words too vulgar for a woman. It startles him.

She presses a button, removes the tape, and turns it over.

He smoothes his hair back with the heel of his hand, a habit from his soldiering days. 'Do you want me to repeat?'

'No,' she says. She presses the 'record' button and the tape whirs. 'Just go on.'

*

The traffic on Prinzregentenplaz was heavy that morning, but Henrich had no trouble finding a place to park. The wealthy inhabitants of the area were working or travelling or driving their cars. They weren't home on a weekday mid-morning, waiting for the Kripo to call.

Fritz counted on that.

He got out of the passenger side, and without waiting for Henrich, mounted the stairs and pushed open the heavy doors with one hand. The hallway was silent, the doors to the offices closed. The scents of leather and boot black were stronger now than they had been the first time, and the silence was eerie.

Henrich came in behind him, eyes wide, saying nothing. He would follow Fritz's lead.

Fritz climbed the formal stairway, a hand on the banister for balance. Dots swam in front of his eyes. He made himself breathe. He had fought in a war with injuries worse than this. Certainly, he could continue an investigation in the same way.

He waited until Henrich was beside him before knocking on the apartment door. He heard a rustling behind the thick wood, then a woman's voice shouted, 'Go away.'

Frau Winter.

'It is Detective Stecher, Frau Winter. Open the door.'

'You are not needed here.'

'No,' he said, 'but we need to talk with you. A man has been killed.'

At that, the door swung open. Fritz placed his meaty palm on the door and slid his boot between the door and the frame. He used his shoulder to push the door wide. Frau Winter blocked him, but he shoved her aside.

'You are not welcome here,' she said.

'I don't care,' he said. 'Where is Herr Hitler?'

'He is not here. I have told you that.'

'So you have,' Fritz said. He nodded to Henrich, who came inside and closed the door. The entry was narrow, not made for three people. 'Where is Frau Dachs?'

'I don't know,' Frau Winter said. She glanced at Henrich, as if she were appealing to his good reason.

'Surely you can lie better than that,' Fritz said. 'Which room is hers?'

Frau Winter did not answer. She crossed her arms, a formidable guard in Hitler's abode.

'Which room?'

'If you do not leave, I will call for help.'

'Like the help that found me last night?'

She bowed her head forward, a tiny acknowledgment of his injuries, and their cause.

★

'She didn't even look startled to see your injuries?' the girl asks.

'No,' he says. 'She knew what had happened to me.'

★

'Stay with her,' he said to Henrich. 'See that she doesn't move.'

'You are making a mistake,' she said.

Fritz turned his back on her, and headed down the hall. As he had suspected, it had been cleaned. The blue carpet looked almost new. He could see the faint blood drops only because he knew where to look.

Geli's door was closed. He turned the glass knob. The door was locked. He had expected as much.

He continued down the hall. Most of the rooms had open

246

doors and closed curtains. It was impossible to tell the time of day. The place smelled of polish and leather mixed with tobacco and wine. The scent of decay was long gone.

Finally he found another closed door. He knocked, then turned the knob. The window was open here, the room flooded with sunlight. Frau Reichert sat inside, huddled in a small chair. An old woman sat beside her, back to the door, staring out the window.

'Go away,' Frau Reichert said. 'Please.'

'Frau Dachs,' Fritz said, ignoring Frau Reichert. 'I am Detective Inspector Stecher. I would like to talk with you about Geli.'

'Please,' Frau Reichert said. 'She is old. She knows nothing.'

'I'd like her to tell me that,' he said. 'Frau Dachs?'

She raised her head, but didn't turn. She was old, and her hair was thinning on top. He could see her pink scalp through wisps of white hair.

'Frau Dachs, I need to know what you saw.'

'She can't tell you,' Frau Reichert said. 'Please.'

Frau Reichert was right. The old woman could tell him nothing. It would be wrong to get her to speak in this house.

'I will take you to the precinct,' he said. 'We will protect you.'

Frau Dachs turned her head slightly. Her skin had softened, fallen in on itself, a cascade of wrinkles.

'Wouldn't you like to leave this house of death?' he asked.

She stood, hand braced on her chair. She too had a dowager's hump. She was frail, but her eyes were bright, sharp, alive.

247

'I would love to,' she said, as if he were asking her to dance.

They left the apartment as quickly as they could, Frau Dachs between them. Frau Reichert was yelling behind them, and Frau Winter had disappeared.

'She will use the telephone,' Frau Dachs said breathlessly. Each step was difficult for her. 'She will call *them*.'

'Whom?' Fritz asked.

'His people. They will stop us.'

'No, they won't,' Henrich said. 'I pulled the telephone from the wall.'

Fritz glared at him over the old woman's head. Henrich shrugged and grinned. 'She wouldn't let go of it. I guess I must have pulled it away too hard.'

When they got to the bottom of the steps, they helped Frau Dachs across the polished floor. Four more steps and they would be to the car. Fritz put his arm around Frau Dachs, wincing as her slight weight pressed against his broken ribs.

'Check,' he said to Henrich.

Henrich went to the door, pushed it open, and looked in both directions. 'Clear to the car,' he said.

Together they half lifted, half pushed Frau Dachs forward. She leaned on Fritz's good arm as they steered her down the steps. They protected her with their bodies as they crossed the sidewalk, and helped her into the back seat.

Fritz slid into the passenger side, and Henrich into the driver's. He took off, heading toward the precinct. Fritz looked over the seat. Frau Dachs was huddled in the back, looking small. Over her shoulder he saw a black car following too close.

'I think Frau Winter contacted someone,' he said.

'She couldn't,' Henrich said. 'I pulled the telephone from the wall.'

The black car was very close. The driver and his passenger were wearing NSDAP uniforms.

'Nonetheless,' Fritz said.

Another car pulled out of a side street. Henrich swerved around it. Frau Dachs ducked.

'They don't have guns, do they?' Henrich asked.

'I don't want to find out,' Fritz said. 'This car has more power. Go!'

Henrich speeded up. He took the next corner so fast that the car wobbled on two wheels. Frau Dachs clung to the back of the seat, her face white. Fritz remained turned, his eyes on the black car. It was fading in the distance. Henrich took another corner, and then an extra.

'Where are you going?' Frau Dachs asked, her voice tremulous.

'The precinct,' Henrich said.

'No,' Fritz said. 'She won't be safe there.'

Henrich turned another corner, and was back on the main road. 'We've had no trouble with the NSDAP there,' he said.

'It doesn't matter,' Fritz said. 'There are Schupo who belong to the NSDAP. Anything could happen.'

'I thought you would protect me,' Frau Dachs said.

'We will,' Fritz said, although he wasn't certain how. They would know his car. They knew his apartment. The Schupo were guarding his apartment, protecting its contents. He and the Chief had set that up the night before. He had nowhere safe to take her.

'We'll go to my apartment,' Henrich said. 'It isn't far. I will give you the keys and take the car to the station. I will bring mine back.'

'Good,' Fritz said. 'Tell the Chief where we are. Tell him we must find somewhere safe for Frau Dachs, and warn him not to tell anyone else.'

'Frau Winter knows you, young man,' Frau Dachs said.

'I'm aware of that,' Henrich said. 'But they'll go to the precinct, then to Fritz's. It will buy us time.'

He pulled the car onto a side street and drove into an alley. Then he stopped behind an old two-storey grey building. He pulled keys from his pocket and handed them to Fritz. 'The second floor,' he said. 'It's the only apartment.'

Fritz got out, then helped Frau Dachs out. As Henrich drove away, she said, 'Can you trust him?'

'I have so far,' Fritz said.

*

'Shouldn't he have stayed?' the girl asks. 'Surely you were in no condition for another fight. You needed some protection.'

'My condition made no difference,' Fritz says. 'If they found us, they wouldn't go after me. They would kill Frau Dachs.'

'Why didn't they, when she was in Hitler's apartment?'

'Because they thought they could keep her quiet. They thought she wasn't a threat.'

'But she was.'

He smiles. 'She was old,' he says, repeating Frau Reichert's words. 'She had nothing to lose.'

THIRTY-SIX

Henrich's apartment was a single room that ran the length of the building. It had a sloped ceiling on both sides. He had hung blankets from one side, making a bedroom area. In the other was a sink and a hot plate, forming a small kitchen. The room was spotless, and warm. It smelled faintly of old wool and mildew. It had no windows, a fact for which Fritz was grateful.

He let Frau Dachs choose her own chair. She picked a rocking chair near the kitchen. He grabbed a straight-backed chair from the table and sat across from her. He had to talk to her quickly. When Henrich returned they would have to take Frau Dachs somewhere else, somewhere safe. By that point, Fritz wanted to know what information he had.

'Forgive my directness,' he said, 'but what is the information they would kill you for?'

Frau Dachs put her small hands on the arms of the rocker, as if bracing herself for what she had to say. 'I watched Adolf Hitler kill Angela Raubal.'

Fritz moved his head back so quickly a dozen bruised muscles screamed. 'You *watched* –?'

251

The woman nodded. 'You have to understand. It never went that far before. We thought it another fight.'

'You weren't alone?' Fritz was still reeling from her first sentence. He had expected to wheedle information from her, to discover that she hadn't known anything at all, or that she only thought something had happened. He hadn't expected her directness.

'My daughter was there. And Frau Winter. Herr Hoffman came up later. He was the one who decided what to do.'

Fritz's mouth was dry. 'Tell me,' he said. 'Tell me everything.'

Frau Dachs's fingers clutched the edge of the chair. She sat as straight as her damaged back would let her. 'We had just finished serving lunch. My daughter was cutting bread in case that man wanted a second serving as he usually did –'

'That man was Hitler?' Fritz asked.

Frau Dachs nodded. She didn't take her gaze off Fritz. 'I do not believe a tyrant should be given the dignity of a name, do you?'

Her hatred was fierce, and startling. No wonder they hadn't let anyone talk with her.

'Your daughter was cutting bread,' Fritz said.

'Yes, and Frau Winter was telling Marlena she was an idiot. Now, Marlena is not smart, but she married a bit of money, and she didn't need to listen to that. I told her so, but she never listened to me as well. The moment I could no longer provide for myself was the moment she stopped listening to me.' Frau Dachs's tone took a bitterness that sounded ingrained. 'I wish she had. We would still be living in our own home instead of following that man around. But

Marlena wanted to live on Prinzregentenplaz. She likes to pretend she is rich.'

Frau Dachs shook her head. 'Sometimes I wonder how I ever begot that girl.'

Fritz would never have called Frau Reichert a girl. He was leaning forward, his back aching, his cracked elbow resting against the chair's wooden arm. The pain was keeping him alert.

'Suddenly, Frau Winter raised her hand for silence. That man and Geli were fighting again. Frau Winter loved to listen. I think it gave her a kind of power. They had been fighting for days. He thought she had a lover in Vienna. She didn't. She went for her music teacher. She thought she could be as famous as her uncle by singing in the cabarets. Silly girl. Geli had gone to Vienna a few days before, but she had got as far as Berchtesgaden when that man called her and demanded that she come home.'

'Hitler's home in Oberstrassburg?' Fritz said. 'She was visiting her mother?'

Frau Dachs nodded. 'Her mother had no idea what to do with Geli. None of us did. And that man spoiled her.'

'I thought you said he beat her,' Fritz said.

Frau Dachs tilted her head. The look she gave Fritz was withering. 'They are not mutually exclusive, young man.'

'No, I suppose not,' Fritz said.

'So, Geli was telling that man that she was going to Vienna, she didn't care what he said. And he was telling her that she couldn't go. She was yelling that she hated being trapped in the apartment, she hated Munich, and she hated

253

his friends. He said she had everything and she should be grateful. She said that she did not have her freedom. She was as trapped as Hansi, her canary.'

Frau Dachs's skin was pale, with two red dots on her cheeks. Although her voice was even, she was not calm. 'And then Geli said she hated being trapped. That man said that if she left, he would make sure she never had anything again. And she said that was fine because she hated him. Then we heard a slap and the sound of breaking dishes. Marlena started to go out, but Frau Winter held her arm.'

Frau Dachs lower lip was shaking. She swallowed before continuing.

'Geli started screaming that he had hurt her. He said he would hurt her worse. We heard more breaking glass and then she started screaming about Hansi. That's when I left the kitchen. I came into the dining hall in time to see him wring the little bird's neck and throw it at Geli. She picked up a knife. She was screaming that he was crazy and that he had killed the only thing she loved. He took out his riding crop and slapped it against his boot and said in that voice he used with her, "Go to your room". She stood in front of him for a minute, blood running down her face, then she turned and ran down the hall. She was still carrying the knife. He followed her. I picked up Hansi and put him in his cage. His little eyes were open, and the bones in his tiny neck were shattered.'

'You didn't go after Geli?'

Frau Dachs shook her head. 'They had fought before. I thought it would end with Hansi's death. After I put him away, I heard them yelling again. I went to the hall to get a broom – Marlena never goes anywhere where there is blood, and Frau Winter was too busy listening. I saw him outside her door. She was waving a knife at him. He had pulled back his coat to show his gun. She said she wasn't afraid of him. He pushed her inside. I was getting frightened. I didn't know if I should call for help or not. I finally decided that I had had enough. I went to his gun cabinet and took out a Walther. He left his guns loaded, fool that he is, and I took it. My hands were shaking, but I figured I could hit that man enough to get him away from her. I got to the door in time to see him grab her by the neck and put his own gun against her chest. I thought he was going to threaten her, but instead he shot her.'

The old woman's hands dropped from the table. She looked down. 'He shot her.'

Fritz's heart was pounding. He could barely speak. But he forced himself to ask, 'Then what, Frau Dachs?'

'I clutched the gun. I thought he was going to kill all of us. But he held her for a moment, then he turned to me. He said, "Frau Dachs, I think I hurt my Geli." I don't think he even saw the gun in my hands. I set the gun down and I went to her. She was dead. By that time, Frau Winter had come in. She looked at that man, then at me, and told us not to move. She went for Herr Hoffman. When she came back, they had already decided they would make it look as if Geli did it herself. Frau Winter made that man change clothes – she took his and burned them – then she and Hoffman made him leave with the chauffeur –'

'Did the chauffeur ever see the body?'

Frau Dachs shook her head. 'Hoffman left it in Frau Winter's hands. I told her I wouldn't lie for him. She told me I would have to. If I didn't, something would happen to me. Marlena was the one who suggested that I say nothing. Pretend I was too distraught.'

She smiled a little.

'I was distraught. Poor child. I close my eyes and I see her bloody face.'

She touched her own face. 'You think it can never go that far, that a woman would die. We all survive it. It is part of the game. But sometimes, sometimes there is one even crazier than we all expect.'

'So Hitler left,' Fritz said, unwilling to listen to the old woman philosophise.

'With Herr Hoffman and the chauffeur, Herr Schreck.'

'What time was that?' Fritz asked.

Frau Dachs shook her head. 'Two-thirty, maybe three. Later than they had planned.'

'Then what happened?'

'Frau Winter called that Hess man, and when he arrived he called Herr Schwarz and Herr Amann. They took Geli, got her to Vienna like she always wanted, made it out to be suicide. No one was to say anything until the next morning. They had that much of a story, but no one knew why she died. They had forgotten that part until the constable showed up.'

Fritz sat up slowly, cautious of his bruises. The timing all made sense to him now. 'So no one called Hitler. He came back the next morning as planned with an alibi, since Geli had shot herself in the middle of the night.'

Frau Dachs nodded. 'He took his gun. Frau Winter put my gun into the poor girl's hand and held it there. Geli was afraid of guns. Perhaps that was the hardest thing, to see them treating her like nothing.'

Fritz took a deep breath. 'Frau Dachs, you saw me, you saw Henrich. You even stayed in the apartment after Hitler came back. You could have spoken to us while we were there. But you did not. Why not? Why did you wait until we came to you?'

She glanced down, her fingers clenched in a fist.

Fritz saw the fear, understood it. 'We won't arrest you, Frau Dachs, for staying silent. You've come forward now. We'll protect you. I just want to know why you waited.'

She took a deep breath, as if saying this next were harder than telling the story. 'Because I did not see a point.'

'There is a point now?'

Frau Dachs nodded. 'I overheard Frau Winter on the phone this morning. She is to make certain that man's clothing is in order. He has a meeting with Hindenburg. She hopes by then he will be over this tragedy.'

'With Hindenburg.' Fritz frowned. He couldn't concentrate as well as he liked. 'What would the President want with him?'

'Some of Hitler's friends want Hindenburg to endorse Hitler for Chancellor.'

'He's not even a German citizen.' Fritz said.

'He is working with a man in Braunschweig to make him

257

a councillor for that state.' Frau Dachs clasped her hands in her lap, as if she were trying to control them.

'Even if that works,' Fritz said, 'no one will ever elect him.'

She pinned him with that intense look. 'No one ever thought the NSDAP would become so powerful in Germany. The second largest party in the Reichstag. If their support grows they will become the largest. Hindenburg will not be able to ignore them then.'

'I am afraid I don't see the connection,' Fritz said. 'Hitler has always been very active politically.'

'I didn't think of it much until Geli died,' Frau Dachs said. 'Then he was so devastated by his actions that I thought he might give it all up. Gregor Strasser is a better man.' She shook her head. 'But I was wrong. That man comes out of these things only stronger. They say he acted the same way after he got those people killed in the putsch. Grief, and guilt and then, suddenly, smarter, stronger. I know what it is like to live with a man like that. I began to think. He loved Geli, in his own way. He loved her. He used the same words to describe her as he uses about Bavaria. I stayed in my room for almost a week, and this morning, when I heard Frau Winter plan his meeting with Hindenburg, I knew.'

'Knew?' Fritz asked.

She nodded. 'I knew. If a man treats the woman he loves that way, imagine. Imagine what he will do if he ever gets control of the country.'

THIRTY-SEVEN

'*She could see it at least,*' the girl says. '*She knew what kind of monster he was.*'

'*But I didn't,*' Fritz says. '*I still thought he was like the rest of us.*'

★

'What will he do, Frau Dachs?' Fritz asked.

She stared at him as if he were insane. 'He will be satisfied with nothing less than complete power. He will treat the country as he treated her. He says he loved her, and he killed her. He will kill us all.' She raised her chin. 'You must stop him. You must stop him now.'

★

Fritz stops. He cannot continue. He is breathing hard. Frau Dachs's words are as painful today as they were then. The girl is watching him, that frown furrowing her forehead. He can't even make an excuse.

'*But you didn't stop him,*' she says. '*You didn't arrest him.*'

'*No,*' he says. '*I did not.*'

She stands. '*You could have saved millions of lives. You!*' *She doesn't seem to remember the tape player running.* '*Don't you think of that?*'

259

'Every day,' he says. His calm tone stops her. She sits, anguish on her face.

'Did you even try?' she asks.

He nods, gropes for the cigarette box, nearly knocking it off the table. He catches it with the other hand, and replaces it. She crouches, takes a cigarette out for him, and hold it out to him. His hands are shaking; he doesn't want to take it. She turns it so that the filter faces him. He puts it in his mouth. She takes his lighter and lights the tip for him. They are so close he can smell the flowery shampoo she uses on her hair.

'Are you all right?' she asks, with more compassion than he deserves.

'Yes,' he says, holding the cigarette tightly between his lips. 'Really.'

The cigarette adds to his light-headedness. She pats his knee, her hand warm, then returns to her chair, once again the prim and proper scholar.

Waiting. Waiting to hear his failure.

'I told you,' he says. 'I told you that sometimes solving the case is not enough. I told you that.'

'You did,' she says.

'We tried.' His voice is soft. 'Henrich came back with the Chief in two separate cars. Henrich took Frau Dachs to a safe place – I never knew where – and the Chief and I talked. He had to find a way around Franz Gürtner. Geli was a suicide. You can't charge a man with murder on a case that's already solved.'

'He failed.'

'Of course. Hitler owned Gürtner. He owned so many.' Fritz set the cigarette on the ashtray. 'But the Chief did take most of the evidence, although he left the paintings with me.'

'Who sent those?'

'We didn't learn until much later. Gregor Strasser, working independently of his brother. They both apparently wanted to take advantage of the situation. Gregor figured that if the police had the paintings, we would investigate Hitler even more.'

'It worked. You investigated.' She is watching his hand as he taps his fingers on the chair. It is as if she is intent on his every movement, as if she is afraid something will happen to him unless she stares.

'Yes,' he says, hating the scrutiny. The room is too hot. A trickle of sweat runs down the back of his neck. His shirt reeks of cigarette smoke and his own body odour. He should have cleaned up before she arrived.

'So it ended where it began, with the Minister of Justice?' She asks the question with such an intensity, he knows she has asked it before. He wonders how long he was quiet. He cannot remember what he was thinking about.

He shakes his head. 'The Chief tried everything he could think of. In a matter of days, he went to the Burgermeister, and the District Committee. None of them wanted to touch the case. Finally, he went to the Minister of the Interior.'

She frowns again. 'The Criminal Police Law of 1922? I thought Bavaria didn't follow it.'

'We followed it, up to a point. We shared information just as we were supposed to, but the state branches remained separate. No state listened to the head of another state. The Minister of the Interior for all of Germany did not want to overturn a ruling by the Bavarian Minister of Justice.'

'Was he corrupt too?' she asks.

Fritz shakes his head. 'Just very smart.'
'So what did the Chief do?'
'It is not what he did. It is what I did.'

THIRTY-EIGHT

His bruises were fading, but driving had been difficult with his injured ribs and elbow. Fortunately, Fritz knew the roads to Berlin. They brought with them memories – memories he hoped would stay buried.

He did not know why he pursued this. The case was closed. Everyone wanted the case to remain closed, except the Chief. He returned the evidence to Fritz and asked him – begged him – to use his fame and his military credentials to get a meeting with Field Marshall Paul von Hindenburg.

★

'I thought Hindenburg collaborated with Hitler.'

Fritz shakes his head. 'It is not as simple as that. Hindenburg was afraid of the Communists. He saw Hitler's people as a buffer, a way to keep the Communists from gaining control of the government. It was logical, given our proximity to Russia, given the fear raised by their revolution. He did not like Hitler, but Hitler was proving himself. And Hindenburg was facing re-election, without a majority. He needed help.'

'You sound sympathetic.'

Fritz sighs. 'Because I understand does not mean I sympathise. I simply know how he thought.'

*

It had been nearly a decade since Fritz had come to Berlin, and then he had been in search of Gisela. This time he stayed away from the cabarets and the hookers, not wanting to see the time-ravaged faces of people he once knew.

Geli had been dead almost a month. The NSDAP stopped harassing Fritz once they thought he was going to leave Hitler alone. Frau Dachs was in her hiding place, and Fritz had his papers in safe storage. The Chief's work had come to nothing. For the first, and only, time in his career, Fritz used his fame to open doors.

And not a moment too soon.

Hitler was due in Berlin the following day. General Kurt von Schleicher, one of Hindenburg's closest advisors, had set up a meeting between Hitler and the President.

Fritz would see Hindenburg first.

Photographers greeted Fritz outside Hindenburg's office. As the bulbs snapped, Fritz suddenly understood why the meeting had been granted. Hindenburg needed the support of a hero, even a press-anointed hero like Fritz. The photographers called Fritz's name, their flashbulbs blinding him and the receptionist so badly that at first he did not see Hindenburg approach.

Hindenburg looked older in person, his face filled with lines and swollen with too much good food and drink. He was shorter than Fritz and stockier, a man for whom middle age was a distant memory. He still moved with power, though, as if years of discipline could not disappear despite the body's deterioration.

Then Hindenburg grabbed Fritz's hand and shook it. He said a few words drowned in the din, and was about to wave good-bye when Fritz grabbed his hand tightly.

Hindenburg's jaw jutted out, given some strength to his elderly beefy face.

'Please, sir,' Fritz said loudly enough for the reporters to hear. 'I would like a moment of your time – in private.'

Hindenburg could not say no to a man whom he had just pretended to be close friends with. He opened the double mahogany doors to his office and let Fritz inside. The doors closed on the photographers, still snapping pictures.

The office was not the one that Hindenburg used for state photographs or official business. It looked like one in which he actually got work done. Photographs from the war years hung on his walls, along with a framed portrait of the Kaiser on his desk. Even though he was president of Germany, Hindenburg was a monarchist at heart.

Hindenburg did not go behind his desk. He stood near the door, forcing Fritz to do the same.

'Forgive me, sir, for taking your time,' Fritz said, 'but I believe this to be very important. I understand you're meeting with Adolf Hitler tomorrow.'

Hindenburg shrugged. 'It is at the request of one of my friends.'

'Sir, I have personal knowledge that Hitler plans to run for election in January, either for your job as President or, more likely, as Chancellor. I mean to stop that.'

Hindenburg smiled and clapped Fritz on the shoulder. 'This is the new Germany. Anyone can run, even a Bohemian corporal.'

'Sir, this Bohemian corporal murdered his own niece.'

Hindenburg's grip on Fritz's shoulder loosened. 'Then you should arrest him.'

'I cannot, sir. The Bavarian Minister of Justice ruled the death a suicide, and no one is willing to overrule him.'

'Then you have wasted your time. I do not get involved in police matters.' Hindenburg took his hand off Fritz's shoulder, and reached for the door.

Fritz pulled the folder he had been carrying out from under his cast. 'The NSDAP bought off the Minister of Justice before the girl's body was cold. When I got too close, they tried to beat me to death. We have a witness who saw Hitler kill the girl, and we have this.'

He opened the folder to show the photographs of Geli's corpse. To his surprise, Hindenburg blushed and looked away.

'Hitler had the body spirited out of Munich the night she died. I went to Vienna and took these. The NSDAP claim she committed suicide. A suicide does not look this.'

'I cannot have the man arrested,' Hindenburg said.

'Yes, you can,' Fritz said. 'And you should, before he sees you. Before he announces that he will run for office. The only time you have is now. Otherwise the NSDAP will discredit your charges as those of a political rival. Right now you can act as President. The entire country believes your word.'

Hindenburg pursed his lips. 'You are considered a great man. I saw your military record. I know of the cases you solved.'

266

Fritz remained still.

'You know what you are asking me?'

'Yes, sir.'

'No, you do not.' Hindenburg's voice rang in the small room. 'You are asking me risk this entire country for your suspicions. The Minister of Justice has ruled. It does not concern me.'

'But it does, sir. You need to know what this man is capable of.'

'You were a soldier, Detective. Are you not capable of the same thing?'

Fritz froze. He felt as if Hindenburg had seen inside his soul.

Are you not capable of the same thing?

The same thing.

And worse.

THIRTY-NINE

'You are nothing like Hitler,' the girl says. 'Nothing.'
Fritz does not look at her.

★

Slowly, very slowly, he took the file from Hindenburg. 'I am sorry to have wasted your time,' Fritz said.

Hindenburg bowed his head slightly. 'It is an honor to meet one of Germany's heroes.'

'I am not one of Germany's heroes,' Fritz said. 'I never have been.'

★

'That's it?' she says. 'You went to Hindenburg and nothing happened?'

'He apparently did not think it was important enough. Perhaps we did not have enough proof. Perhaps the unorthodox nature of the investigation made him leary.'

'But you let it end there. And then you ran away.'

'I did not run away,' Fritz says.

'You left. You left Germany. You had the power to change history and you did not use it.'

'Tell me how I could have.' His voice is low. Mean. He does not let himself move. He knows he cannot. 'You seem to know all. You tell me how I could have.'

'You could have brought the information to the press.'

'The press already had the information. They did nothing.'

'You could have given the information to the Strassers, let them fight it out within the NSDAP.'

'They already had the information too. Gregor Strasser lost his power struggle with Hitler. Within a year, he resigned.'

'Then you should have taken it to the foreign press.'

'Why?' Fritz says. 'They could have done nothing. They knew of the violence against Jews. They even knew of the camps. If that didn't stop Hitler, this murder of a single girl could not have either.'

'Then why did you tell me about it?'

He stops, takes a breath. The air in the room is close, and smells of sweat, and fear. She is afraid of him, afraid of his anger.

As she should be.

'You asked,' he says. 'You want to know the mind of a detective and how it solves crimes.'

'Yes, but I had Demmelmayer. I did not need this.'

'But you did,' he says. 'You need to know how a detective's mind works, both for him and against him. I failed on this case, but not where you think.'

She crosses her arms. 'Where, then?'

'I underestimated the man I faced. From the start, I underestimated him. I would have acted differently if I had known how much power he already had.'

'You would have turned down the case.'

'Perhaps,' he says. His fists are shaking. 'You no longer respect

270

me, do you? I am a failure to you. The man who could have stopped Hitler.'

She is standing, packing her things with excitement. She is like a reporter on a hot story, ready to send the lead to her paper. 'How can you live with yourself?'

'That is the question, isn't it?' he says.

She looks at him, her eyes narrowed in contempt. She picks up the last of her things, shakes her head, and then she disappears out his door.

He sits.

He doesn't move until the apartment gets dark. He stares at the door, expecting it to open again, expecting her to come back, to understand. He has just emptied himself to her, and she rejected him, and all he tried.

She didn't understand after all.

He is not sure he does.

Finally, he gets up. He picks up the phone, begins to dial, and puts it down. He cannot. He cannot be alone, but he cannot have company.

He goes into the bedroom, with his ghosts.

As he flicks on the light he sees the photographs where he left them. He picks up the last, the clipping taped to cardboard. Gisela's face stares back at him, her eyes ringed in kohl, her leg up, showing the shapeliness of her thigh. The stocking is perfect, its seam a straight line down the back of her leg. The sailor who bends over her has his hand on her breast.

The caption reads, in English, 'Berlin matrons sell sex for bread'.

He found the clipping during his exile in London after the Raubal case broke. He ripped it out of a book on the history of

271

inflation in Germany after the war. Then he went from library to library, tearing out that page, so that no one else would see his wife that way. No one had to know the depths her desperation took her.

And him.

He hears a sound behind him, a latch catching, footsteps.

'Fritz?'

He gets up, his breath caught in his throat. Her voice has a tremble of worry, as if she thinks he won't forgive her. He sets the clipping on the bed and comes out of the room.

She stands in the light. 'I'm sorry,' she says. 'I had to come back. I don't know what came over me —'

He flies from the bedroom and grabs her by the throat, shoving her against the wall. 'It is too late,' he says. She is flailing at him with her fists. They don't hurt. She has no strength. 'You think you can come back now? It is too late.'

She coughs and he lets her throat go. She rubs it, then looks up at him and opens her mouth. He slaps her before she has a chance to say a word. He cannot hear her apologies. Not now. Not after so long. He went through it all too. He did. She has to understand that.

'Fritz,' she says, her voice rasping. She brings up a hand to protect her face.

'You cannot come back here. You don't belong here. You left!'

She pushes herself against the wall, uses her one hand to lever herself up. He reaches out to strike her again, but she catches his wrist.

'Fritz, it's Annie. Annie. The American. Annie. You know?'

She has a new name now. She comes back, older, used, expecting him to forgive her, and she has a new name. Damn her. Didn't she know that he needed her then as much as she needed him? They all starved. His children died too.

272

They all died together.

He wrenches his hand free. He will teach her to deny him, to turn her back on him.

'My God,' she says. 'Who do you see? Who do you see when you look at me?'

'Gisela,' he says. 'Stop this.'

'My name is Annie,' she repeats. 'I am from Boston. Harvard. You spent the last few days telling me about Geli Raubal.'

Geli's name makes him freeze. Geli. Gisela did not know about her. He gropes for the light switch, turns on the lights. Annie's cheek is swelling.

'I hurt you,' *he says, his voice small.*

He had said the same thing to Gisela, only she had not moved. He had gone to her, held her in his arms, and she had still not moved.

Annie is cringing. She is keeping her body as far away from his as she can.

He does not blame her.

He goes into the kitchen, gets ice, and wraps it in a cloth, then hands it to her. His fingers left bruises on her neck.

She takes the cloth and presses it against her cheek. 'Who is Gisela?'

'My wife.'

Annie pushes away from the wall, and goes into the kitchen, away from him. 'I came to see if you were all right. I shouldn't have left that way. You have been living alone with this. You needed to tell someone —'

'I am not well,' *he says.* 'I hurt you.'

'We need to get you help.'

She is different from anyone he has ever met. The hooker he beat up cringed from him. Gisela ran away, and he went to the police academy to learn discipline.

'I am too old for help.'

'Nonsense,' she says, but she does not come any closer to him. She keeps her distance. Always will, now. 'No one is too old for help.'

'I am.' He picks up the chair he knocked over in his rush from the bedroom.

'Hindenburg said you were a hero,' she says. 'You are one of the most brilliant detectives of all time. This has to be some kind of stress —'

'I am not a hero,' he says. 'I am like them.'

'Them?'

'Demmelmayer. Hitler. I am like them.'

'You are nothing like that. You didn't kill your wife.'

His breath catches in his throat. He turns from her, unable to look at her bruises, at the face so similar to Gisela's. He staggers to his chair, the place where he confesses.

'You asked,' he says. 'You asked what makes a detective great.'

She remains by the door.

'You asked.'

It is why he no longer sleeps. He cannot bear to see Gisela's face imprinted on all those other faces, her nose broken like Geli's, her voice pleading with him like the hooker's.

'It is the secret, you know,' he says. 'You all come, looking for that secret. How does the great detective solve his cases? He solves them by understanding the criminal mind. By possessing one himself.'

'You're distraught,' she says.

'No.' He backs away from her, keeping the chair between them.

'I finally understand. Frau Dachs was right. A tyrant is a man who destroys the people around him. Like Demmelmayer did. Like Hitler did. Like me.'

'You are nothing like Hitler,' she says again. 'He killed millions.'

Fritz studies his hands. Unfamiliar hands. Hands with great strength. Enough strength to close on a woman's neck and choke the life from her.

'He started,' Fritz says slowly, 'with the woman he loved.'

She takes the cloth from her cheek. Her eyes are dark; Gisela's were blue. She is thin, but fashionably so. Gisela was bony with starvation. Her hair is more blonde than brown. Gisela was a brunette. They do not look alike in any way.

Her face knows joy. Gisela's never did.

He wonders how many years it has been since he saw women as themselves, and not as Gisela.

How many years since he saw himself with any kind of clarity.

He doubts he ever did.

Annie is watching him. Her eyes hold a compassion he does not deserve. 'You never told that story about Hitler to anyone else,' she says. 'Why now?'

'It needs to be told. Someone needs to remember.'

'But why did you tell it to me?'

He looks at her, the poorly dressed daughter of a country he does not understand, with her need, her desires, her fears etched on her features like writings on glass. The fact that she stands in his kitchen after he has hurt her shows that she has more courage than he has ever had in all of his life.

'Why did you tell me?' she asks again.

'Because,' he says, 'I was hoping that someone would forgive me.'

'For Hitler?'

He shakes his head. 'Many of us share the blame for that. No. For Gisela.'

'You killed her?' She sounds like she does not believe, like she cannot.

'Like I nearly killed you.' He stands, gets out of the confessional and goes to the window. Then he waves his hand at the bedroom door. 'The box in there. It has the whole story. You tell it all. You tell the world about the mind of a man who catches great criminals. You tell them. But you tell them that catching them is not enough. You must stop them.'

He leans his head against the cool glass. 'I could not even stop myself.'

The apartment is silent. When he turns, she is gone. Perhaps she thought he meant to kill her. He did not. Gisela was his last victim.

Except for the indirect ones. The ones he failed when he fled Hindenburg's office, when he disappeared from Germany for decades.

Millions of victims.

How can he live with this?

Because he has to. Because death will bring no peace. They wait for him on the other side, their faces blurred and indistinct. Only Gisela's face will be clear. Gisela, gaunt and starving, surviving only as she knew how, making the best of a world in which nothing remained.

He leans his head on the glass. He can see the street below, see the American girl running to her cab. She flees him like he fled Germany.

'Running is not the answer,' he whispers. 'Closing your eyes is not the answer.'

For what she fails to realise is that he is not unique. Demmelmayer was not unique.

And neither was Hitler.

Perhaps that is what Fritz was trying to tell her. Perhaps that is what he wanted her to see. How easily monsters are formed –

– and how difficult it is to stop them.

AUTHOR'S NOTE

Angela Maria Raubal, Adolf Hitler's half-niece and the so-called love of his life, died in his apartment in the middle of September in 1931. Her body was removed before the police arrived. She was ruled a suicide, but buried in consecrated ground in Vienna. The priest, Father Pant, is said to have believed that Geli Raubal was murdered.

Hitler's inner circle provided his alibi. The press did not believe it. The articles quoted here did appear in local papers, as did Hitler's denial. The theories floated here are theories about Geli Raubal's death. But that's as far as it goes. Fritz is my character, and his actions and interactions are all fiction.

History's mass murderers are not born full-blown psychopathic adults. They were children. They had histories of their own. They left trails of earlier victims. If the Munich police had conducted a real investigation, if the Minister of Justice had not ruled Geli's death a suicide (a decision made as a political favour to the NSDAP), Adolf Hitler would have been arrested for murder – and millions of lives would have been saved.